WYOMING'S MOST ELIGIBLE BACHELORS

1. Chad Randall
2. <u>Pete Randall</u>
3. Brett Randall
4. Jake Randall

<u>Cons</u>	<u>Pros</u>
hard-hearted	good-lookin'
mule-headed	hot-blooded
love 'em & leave 'em	rough & ready

No contest—the Randall brothers are the best catch in the county!

Their response: "Wild horses can't make us take a wife!"

Dear Reader,

Last month Jake Randall stopped at nothing to get little brother Chad married off—but he's not content to stop there! He wants Pete and Brett to follow Chad down the aisle, then populate the Randall ranch with herds of little ones. This month, and in the months ahead, you'll read all about this family in my new miniseries, 4 BRIDES FOR 4 BROTHERS!

I love big families who care about each other and I love cowboys. Out there on their Wyoming ranch, the Randall brothers fill both bills. As oldest brother and keeper of the family, Jake feels responsible for the fact that none of his brothers has married, so he sets out to play Cupid for them. Like most big brothers, he thinks he knows best. And like most younger brothers, Chad, Pete and Brett don't cooperate! Their stories will make you laugh out loud and make you want to join the Randalls in their pursuit of love.

I hope you'll join me at the Randall brothers' ranch for all four books in the 4 BRIDES FOR 4 BROTHERS series!

Happy reading!

Judy Christenberry

Judy Christenberry

COWBOY DADDY

Harlequin Books

TORONTO • NEW YORK • LONDON
AMSTERDAM • PARIS • SYDNEY • HAMBURG
STOCKHOLM • ATHENS • TOKYO • MILAN
MADRID • WARSAW • BUDAPEST • AUCKLAND

ISBN 0-373-16653-2

COWBOY DADDY

Copyright © 1996 by Judy Christenberry.

This edition published by arrangement with Harlequin Books S.A.

® and TM are trademarks of the publisher. Trademarks indicated with ® are registered in the United States Patent and Trademark Office, the Canadian Trade Marks Office and in other countries.

Printed in U.S.A.

Chapter One

He was tall, broad shouldered, and his tan face was turned down in a frown. Janie Dawson had worked hard to prepare for this meeting, girding her strength. But one look at the cowboy standing in his living-room doorway told her no mental exercise could have toughened her enough to face Pete Randall.

"Hi, Pete," she croaked out.

He wasted no time on amenities. "What are you doing here?"

Her eyebrows rose at his directness. She'd been a neighbor of the Randalls since her birth. As a child, she'd been in and out of their house countless times. As a teenager, she'd followed Pete Randall around with all the adoration of a young girl for her idol. As a woman, she'd been his lover.

But now she evidently needed a good reason for being there.

"I wanted to talk to you."

His hands rested on his trim hips, and his brown-eyed gaze stayed on her face. "As I remember, three weeks ago you told me you never wanted to speak to me again."

She felt her cheeks heat up. He was right, of course. Three weeks ago, she'd decided she'd made a mistake, a big mistake, believing Pete's desire for her meant he loved her. Instead, it had meant exactly what it was—lust.

As long as she could remember, she'd loved Pete Randall. When he'd finally noticed her as a woman, all grown up, she'd fallen into his arms, ready to follow wherever he led.

He'd led her straight to bed.

Six months later, when she'd finally woken up from the sexual haze his touch brought about, she'd realized she wasn't his love but his lover.

Her teeth sank into her bottom lip. "Yes, I did." She walked across the room to the front window and stared out at the cold Wyoming day.

From behind her, his voice deepened. "So, what's changed?"

She turned around before he could come too near, a fixed smile on her face. "I think I was a little hasty."

A flame in his brown eyes ignited, and a lazy grin lit his face. "You mean you want to come back to me?"

She'd had her game plan worked out, but the fluttering of her heart at his question almost shook her. With a deep breath, she clung to her goal. "No, that's not what I mean."

His gaze hardened again. "Then what?"

She stuck her fingers in the back pockets of her jeans so he wouldn't see them shaking. "I wanted to ask you a question."

He folded his arms across his chest. "Ask away."

Easier said than done. She swallowed and shifted her gaze from his. She could get the words out better if she wasn't looking at him. "I wanted to ask you— ask you to marry me."

The taut silence that followed her question forced her gaze back to his well-loved features. A mixture of shock and panic filled his face.

She wasn't surprised by his reaction. She'd been pretty sure he wouldn't consider her offer. The Randall brothers, all four of them, were notorious bachelors. They had all resisted marriage since the marriage of the oldest brother, Jake, had ended in divorce.

"Have I shocked you?" she finally asked when he failed to answer.

He nodded as he moved toward her. "Yeah, you have. Look, Janie, I told you from the beginning I wasn't— I had no intention of— I care about you, Janie."

"But you don't love me." She stated her conclusion with finality, having expected no less. It was a struggle to keep a smile on her face, but she did.

His big hand caressed her cheek.

"Sweetheart, I wouldn't do anything to hurt you but—but I'm not cut out for marriage. You know that."

His touch almost destroyed her composure. She stepped back from him. "Yes, I know."

An awkwardness filled the room. When she thought she could bear the silence no longer, she stepped around him and walked to the door. "Sorry

I interrupted your work," she tossed over her shoulder, glad she didn't have to face him again.

"Janie, wait."

She ignored his command. If she stayed any longer, she wouldn't be able to keep her smile in place.

"Janie, why?"

That question stopped her in her tracks. Why not tell him? He'd have to find out sometime. And she already had the answer to her question. Turning, she stiffened her shoulders, pasted on her brightest smile and said, "Because I'm having your baby."

Then she left the room.

PETE STOOD without moving, stunned, like the time Joe Bob Daly had broken Pete's nose in his first fight. Only Janie's disappearance awakened him.

"Wait!" he called, but he didn't rely on his voice to bring her to heel. After all, he knew Janie well. Instead, he hurried after her into the entry hall, catching her by the arm and pulling her back when she would've left the house.

"Where do you think you're going?" he growled.

"Home." She flashed him that breezy smile she'd been using the past half hour.

"You drop a bombshell like that and then plan on waltzing home?" he demanded, outrage rising in his voice as the shock retreated.

"Well, it's a little early for a formal announcement. What else do you want from me?"

She sounded so reasonable, as if she'd announced she was dying her hair. Instead, she'd said she was...having his baby. It almost took his breath away.

"Well?" she said, her hands on her slim hips, her smile slipping a little.

"Why didn't you tell me?" he finally asked.

Her brows soared. "I just did."

"When did you find out? Have you been to the doctor?"

"I've suspected for a few days," she admitted, running a finger along the edge of the hall table, not meeting his gaze. "I saw Doc Jacoby yesterday."

Pete knew there must be a thousand questions to ask, but he was too overwhelmed. Finally he managed to say, "When...?"

"Is it due?" she finished for him. "August."

"And everything is all right?"

"Oh, yes. I'm healthy as can be." She didn't wait for any more questions. Turning toward the door, she said, "I have to go now."

"Wait!" he repeated, grabbing her arm again. "We have to make plans."

"For what?"

"For our marriage, for one thing," he said, wondering if pregnancy affected the brain. A discussion of future plans should've been obvious.

"No, that's not necessary."

That damn plastic smile was back in place, and she wasn't making any sense. "Of course it's necessary. We've both got family to invite...and friends... and..."

"There's not going to be a wedding, Pete," Janie said softly. "That's why we don't need to make plans."

He almost stumbled back at the second blow Janie had delivered. "What are you talking about? Of course there's going to be a wedding!"

She shook her head, her stubborn little chin rising as it always did when she was digging in her heels. Then she reminded him, "You turned me down, remember?"

Suddenly her earlier behavior made sense. "Yeah, but you didn't tell me *why* you asked me to marry you."

"In my book, there's only one reason to ask or accept. And it's not a baby."

"Well, it should be! I'm not having my son born a bastard, thinking I didn't care enough to marry his mother!"

"You do what you want . . . but I'm not marrying you," she returned rapid fire.

"Why?" Pete demanded.

"Because you don't love me, Pete. You want me . . . but you don't love me. That's not enough for marriage." For the first time, her smile disappeared and unshed tears filled her blue eyes. This time, before he could stop her, she left.

He stared at the closed door, rational thought almost impossible. Janie's bombshells left him too distraught. After several minutes, he turned to the back of the house, automatically heading for the kitchen, the gathering place for his family.

Red, the cowboy-turned-cook who'd taken care of him and his three brothers since his mother's death twenty-six years ago, was working at the sink. "Janie gone?"

"Yeah." Pete pulled out a chair at the long breakfast table.

"You okay?" Red asked as he reached the table, two mugs of steaming coffee in his hands. He set one in front of Pete and then pulled out the chair across from him.

"I don't know." Pete studied the dark liquid and then looked at Red. "Janie's pregnant."

Red's eyes widened, but he said nothing.

"I don't understand women at the best of times, Red, but pregnant women don't make any sense."

"Don't look at me for advice, boy. I've chased a few pregnant cows in my time, and there's not an ornerier animal alive. But pregnant women? I'm just as lost as you."

The two men sat in silence before Red ventured another question. "Is the baby yours?"

"Of course it is! We'd been— We started going out a few months ago."

"No offense meant, Pete." Red sipped his coffee before grinning. "Jake's gonna be ridin' high. Ever since he matched up Chad and Megan, he's been thinkin' how he'll find wives for you and Brett, too. Now the only bachelor will be Brett."

Pete drew a painful breath. "She says she won't marry me."

The older man stared at him as if he'd lost his mind. "What? That's crazy. If you don't marry her, her dad'll be over here with a shotgun!"

"I know."

"Is she gonna marry that greenhorn?" Red suddenly asked, sitting up straight in his chair.

Pete froze. He hadn't had time to think about why Janie had turned him down. At least not in terms of another man. After Janie had sent him away three weeks ago, she'd been seen around town with a man who had recently moved to Wyoming from Chicago. He shook his head. "She can't!"

"Well, sonny, I reckon she can. There's no law against it."

"Damn it! Some greenhorn isn't gonna raise my boy! I won't put up with that!" Pete leapt to his feet and began pacing the large kitchen. "That's just not gonna happen!"

"Don't rant and rave at me, boy. I'm not the one cramping your style," Red protested, scarcely moving.

"Who's cramping Pete's style?" Jake asked from the doorway as he shed his winter coat and Stetson.

Brett, the third of the Randall brothers, was right behind Jake. Before either Red or Pete could answer Jake's question, Brett asked, "Where's Janie?"

Pete felt an almost-unheard-of urge to lie to his brother, but Brett was the one who had brought word to the barn that Janie was here to see him. He wouldn't believe she'd been abducted by space aliens. "Janie's gone."

"What'd she want?"

Glaring at Brett, Pete mumbled, "Nothing."

"You gotta tell 'em sometime," Red said.

"Tell us what?" Jake asked, taking a step toward Pete.

Pete hated to face Jake. He recognized the concern in his big brother's face, heard the worry in his voice. Jake took his role as oldest brother and head of the family very seriously.

And he really wanted another generation of Randalls to carry on the tradition of the ranch.

"Janie—Janie wanted to talk to me," Pete began, trying to figure out how to explain his situation.

"No kidding, Sherlock," Brett drawled as he poured coffee for himself and Jake, who'd already taken a seat at the table.

Pete shot him another glare before returning to the table and sitting down. "Janie's pregnant."

A quick look at his brothers' faces made him think he should've broken the news to them more slowly. He cleared his throat to try again.

Jake beat him to the punch. Leaping to his feet, he grabbed Pete's hand. "Congratulations, Pete! That's great! Janie's a terrific girl. We've started building on the next generation. I didn't expect it to happen this fast. I mean, Chad and Megan just got married. The most I'd hoped for was a baby by this time next year. But already pregnant! When are you going to have the wedding? It should be soon so people won't talk too much."

By this time, Jake had abandoned Pete's hand and was pacing the kitchen, excitedly making plans.

"Jake," Pete said.

"We can have the wedding here. Though I guess Hank and Lavinia might want it at their house. We'll need to call Chad and Megan so they can get back here in time. What about—?"

"Jake!" Pete roared.

"What?" Jake returned with a frown.

"She refused to marry me."

While Jake stared at Pete, shock all over his face, Brett asked, "Is it your baby?"

"Of course it's my baby!"

"Well, it could be that greenhorn's, you know. They've been going out."

"For just three weeks! She's seven or eight weeks along." Actually he was pretty sure of the exact night when she'd gotten pregnant. They'd had words, and the making-up had been passionate.

Jake slowly returned to his chair. "Then why won't she marry you?"

"She—she tricked me."

"Tricked you? You mean by getting pregnant?" Jake demanded.

"No! She didn't do that on purpose. And we used protection every time," Pete hastily added. Jake had made sure all his brothers understood their responsibilities. "She asked me to marry her before she told me she was pregnant. You know I don't—didn't—intend to marry. And—and I said no."

"So tell her you changed your mind," Jake said, impatience in his voice.

"I did. But she wouldn't listen."

"Man, old Hank is gonna be on your back tighter than a tick on a hound dog," Brett said.

"Yeah," Pete agreed. "But unless he can handle his stubborn daughter better than me, I don't know what we'll do about it."

"MOM, WE NEED TO TALK," Janie said as she entered the kitchen. She dreaded the conversation she had to have with her mother, but she needed to get it over with. Her stomach wasn't too happy right now, and tension only seemed to make it worse.

"Sure, hon. We can talk while I mix this cake. Betty Kelsey broke her hip, and I thought I'd take a few things over for their dinner."

"I'm sorry to hear about Betty." She'd tried to sound sincere even though it was hard to think about anyone else's woes right now when hers seemed so large. And the smell of that perfectly innocent cake batter was making her nauseous.

Lavinia frowned. "Is something wrong?"

Janie used the same smile she'd practiced on Pete. "I guess you could say that."

Lavinia abandoned her baking and sat down at the table beside her daughter. Covering Janie's hand with hers, she was the epitome of a concerned mother. Janie knew she was lucky to have her parents. Which made the disappointment she was going to bring them even more difficult.

"There's no easy way to tell you, Mom, except to say I'm sorry."

"Janie, what is it?" Suddenly Lavinia crossed her arms over her chest and grinned. "Did you gain a few pounds and that expensive suit you bought last week won't fit?"

"Not yet. But I probably will soon," she offered, a small laugh accompanying her words.

"Then what is it?"

"I'm pregnant."

Lavinia's hand tightened momentarily on Janie's before she put it in her lap to clasp her hands tightly together. "I—I see. May I ask who's the father?"

"Of course you can, Mom. It's Pete."

Relief filled Lavinia's face. "Oh. That's all right, then. Pete will do the right thing."

Janie heaved a big sigh. "Yes, he will, Mom, but I won't."

"What do you mean? Lavinia Jane Dawson, surely you're not thinking of an abortion?"

"No! I intend to have my baby. But I'm not going to marry Pete." She looked away from her mother's inquiring stare.

"I don't understand."

"I love Pete, Mom, but he doesn't love me. He offered to marry me when he found out I was pregnant. But five minutes earlier, he refused to marry me. I won't trap him into marriage just because—because I'm carrying his child."

Her hand rested on her stomach. Somehow the words hadn't seemed true until this moment. She was carrying Pete's child. Forever she would have a part of him in her life. She faced her mother with another smile, this one warm and real. "I don't know what you and Daddy want. I mean, I don't want to embarrass you. If you want me to go away, I will."

"You'll do no such thing, Janie," Lavinia assured her, reaching over to enclose her daughter in a hug. "You're our daughter and you'll have your baby here. If you choose to be an unwed mother, you'll need our help."

"I can manage, Mom. I'll move to Casper and get a job. People will talk if I don't marry." Janie didn't want to be selfish, taking her comfort while causing her parents pain.

"Absolutely not! I'm not having my grandbaby born in Casper! Raised as a city kid? Why, she'd probably grow up and join a gang!"

"Mother! In Casper?" Janie couldn't help laughing, though her eyes were clouded with tears.

"You just never know. No, we'll keep the Dawsons here on the ranch, all of us, where we belong."

"Mom, you're so wonderful. Are you sure?"

"I'm sure. Now, are you going to tell anyone who the father is? Or did you want to keep it secret?"

"I guess that's up to Pete. Dr. Jacoby asked me if I knew the father but—"

"He did what? Did he think you'd sleep with someone you didn't know? Of all the nerve! Wait until I get my hands on him."

"Mom," Janie said, touching her mother's arm, "you'll have to expect that kind of reaction. Are you sure you don't think it would be best if I went away?"

Lavinia settled back down in her chair. "No, you won't go away, and I don't want to hear another word. And I'll try to restrain myself, but I can't believe Fred Jacoby would—"

"Mom, it's okay. Anyway, I told him I knew who the father was but I'd rather not say."

"And did you and Pete discuss—I mean, what did he say?"

"He said he'd marry me." Janie closed her eyes, fighting the pain of turning him down.

"And you said no?"

She nodded.

"Did you discuss—?"

"Nothing. I—I had to leave. I didn't want him to feel sorry for me."

The two women sat in silence until the roar of a truck approaching the house roused them.

"Daddy! That's him, isn't it?" Janie asked. "What are we going to tell him?"

"Well, we'll have to tell him the truth sometime, sweetheart. You know he loves you."

"Yes, I know, but I don't think he'll take it too well. Could we wait just a little while? It won't matter. I'm sure Pete won't tell anyone for a while, if ever." She couldn't bear the thought of facing her father with her news.

"Okay, we'll wait... until an opportune moment arrives, when your father's calm."

Janie almost laughed. With that criterion, she'd have to keep her news from her father a very long time. She only hoped he had a calm moment before she started showing. Otherwise, the roof would come off the house.

The back door swung open, and Hank Dawson strode into the kitchen. In spite of her distress, Janie smiled at the energy that filled the room when he entered. Her mother was the center of the tornado, calm, cool, serene. Her father was the tornado, blustery, quick, powerful.

"Hello there, ladies!" he boomed as he walked to the wall phone. Without any other words, he dialed, then waited impatiently. Abruptly he hung up the phone.

"Damn, line's busy. Well, I'll be back in half an hour, Lavinia, and I'll be plenty hungry." He patted Janie's shoulder and dropped a kiss on Lavinia's lips before starting for the door.

"Where are you going?" Lavinia asked.

"To the Randalls'. I've got to talk to Pete. Some of his herd has escaped."

Before Janie could voice a protest at his destination, he was out the door, already getting into his pickup truck.

"I hope you're right about Pete keeping quiet, Janie. I sure would hate for your father to find out about the baby from Pete."

"You and me both," Janie agreed, rolling her eyes. The explosion such an event would occasion might make the citizens of Wyoming think they were experiencing their first major earthquake.

Chapter Two

The three Randall brothers and Red were still sitting around the kitchen table, trying to sort out the situation, when they heard a truck coming down the long driveway.

"Who could that be?" Brett asked, and stood to walk to the kitchen window. "Damn! It's Hank. Janie must've already told him!"

Everyone stood, though none of them seemed to know what to do.

Jake placed his hand on Pete's arm. "You'd better stay here. I'll go talk to Hank."

"Nope. It's my problem. I'll deal with it, Jake." He wasn't looking forward to this conversation, but Pete wasn't about to hide behind his brother's coattails. Besides, he'd offered to do the right thing. It was Janie who'd refused.

Pete strode to the door, reaching for his coat hanging beside it, but Hank opened the back door before he could intercept him.

"Howdy, boys. I woulda called, but your line was busy. Just wanted to warn you."

"Look, Hank, the others don't have anything to do with this."

"I know that, Pete, but—"

"Why don't we go outside and talk?" Pete suggested, desperate to avoid having an audience, even if it was his brothers and Red.

"Outside in the cold? You must have feathers for a brain, son. It's twenty degrees out there. What we have to talk about isn't *that* world bending."

Pete stared at him. The man didn't think his daughter getting pregnant was important? "Hank, I promise I didn't intend for this to happen."

"'Course you didn't. Accidents do happen," he assured him with a grin. "I know you'll take care of it."

"Well, I tried."

"Oh, so you already knew about the problem?"

"Yeah. But just today."

"Then everything's settled. And I won't protest if one or two of my little ones look a lot like a Randall brand."

Pete couldn't believe what he was hearing. "That's it?" he asked.

"Well, if the little mama gets ornery, I may send her over to you to take care of until after she delivers. How about that?"

"Hank, didn't she tell you? I'm willing to marry her," Pete said in a strangled voice.

Hank's genial smile disappeared, and his brows lowered. "What are you talking about?" he demanded.

"Janie. What were you talking about?"

"Janie? Why were we talking about Janie? I was talking about your bulls getting into my herd and—" Hank's eyes widened, and his face turned a mottled red. "You got Janie pregnant?" he roared, and started toward Pete.

Jake quickly moved between them. "Now, Hank, wait just a minute. Pete offered to marry Janie. She's the one who said no."

"She said what? Well, that don't excuse Pete. He shouldn'ta been messing with Janie! My little girl! How dare you, boy?" He tried to push past Jake.

Brett joined Jake in his attempts to calm Hank. Pete almost wished they'd move aside and let Hank do his worst. Maybe it would assuage the guilt Pete felt.

"Hank!" Jake protested. "Pete didn't do it by himself. Janie's a grown woman. She didn't have to fight him off, you know."

"Are you sure?" Hank growled.

Jake stepped back, and Brett with him. "You ought to know better than that, Hank."

"Hell, I didn't mean any insult," Hank assured him, his gaze seeking Pete's over Jake's shoulder. "So why haven't you been to see me, to settle things man-like? That's what your dad woulda wanted."

"Because Janie just told me this afternoon, about an hour ago. As soon as she told me, I asked her to marry me, but she turned me down. We were just trying to figure out what to do." Pete paused and then added, "I'm sorry, Hank. I wouldn't have hurt you and Lavinia for anything."

"How about Janie? I imagine she's going to be hurt the worst," Hank said, sadness replacing his anger.

"Hank, I swear I'm perfectly willing to marry her and take care of her and the baby."

"Fine. Then we'll make the arrangements. And we won't have any hide-in-the-closet kind of marriage, either. Our Janie is our pride and joy."

"With good reason," Pete agreed, smiling slightly for the first time. "She's a wonderful woman."

"Yeah," Hank agreed. But his voice was faint, and he suddenly reached for a chair. "Janie pregnant," he muttered. Suddenly he looked up at Pete, his gaze sharpening. "I didn't even know you two were seeing each other." Before Pete could say anything, he asked another question. "Didn't you think about the consequences?"

"Of course I did. But, like you said, accidents happen."

Silence fell, and the Randalls and Red joined Hank at the table. Jake leaned forward. "Hank, Pete says Janie refused him. Are you sure you can change her mind?"

"Of course I can," Hank assured them, straightening his shoulders. "Janie always does what I tell her to do."

With that statement, Pete realized he knew Janie better than her father did. And he also came to the conclusion that the next few days were going to be difficult.

"Why'd she turn you down?" Hank asked, swinging his gaze to Pete.

He ran his finger around the collar of his shirt. "Uh, she asked me to marry her before she told me she was pregnant."

"And?"

"I said no."

"You've been sleeping with her but you didn't think she was good enough to marry?" From the sound of his voice, Hank's hackles were up again.

"Hank! You know better than that. It's not Janie who's the problem. She's—she's wonderful." He paused to clear his throat. "I never planned to marry. After Jake's—" his gaze flicked to his older brother, hating the regret he read there "—divorce, I decided I didn't need that kind of pain. But the baby—" Again he broke off. Just saying those words threw him for a loop. "The baby makes a difference."

"Did you tell Janie that?" Hank retorted.

Pete drew a deep breath and then exhaled. "She didn't give me a chance. I tried to make some plans, and she said they weren't necessary because she wasn't going to marry me. Then she left."

Hank rose to his feet. "Well, I guaran-damn-tee you there'll be a wedding before my first grandchild takes a breath, so get your best suit pressed, boy. You're about to become a member of my family." Then he strode out of the room without saying good-bye.

Jake was the first to speak. "Do you think he'll convince her?"

Pete shrugged his shoulders.

"Well, I remember Janie's stubbornness," Brett threw in. "I have my doubts."

Pete stood. "We'll find a way. My baby is too important." He left the kitchen in a hurry, as if he needed to be outside to breathe.

"Man, I hope he's right," Jake muttered. Then he looked at Brett. "And if he is, and he and Janie marry, you'd better start looking for a likely bride for youself, too, 'cause you'll be next on my list."

"Hey, Jake, two out of three ought to satisfy you," Brett protested.

"Nope. I want all my brothers married with lots of little Randalls underfoot. And don't you forget it."

JANIE HAD TROUBLE concentrating on any of her chores as she waited for her father's return. Even if Pete kept quiet, she needed to tell her father that she was pregnant.

He'd be upset. Unlike her mother's reaction, her father would explode. And his anger wouldn't all be directed at Pete. Rightly so. In fact, if she was honest with herself, she was probably more responsible than Pete.

After all, what single man, when faced with one hundred percent cooperation, wouldn't take a reasonably attractive, single young woman to bed? And she'd been totally cooperative. She'd loved Pete for so long, it had seemed natural to melt into his arms, to let passion surge between them.

But she'd been wrong.

Now she had to face her father and explain to him why she'd made this mistake...and why she wouldn't marry Pete.

The phone rang and Janie, in her father's office doing some of the paperwork that weighed down a rancher, stared at it. Was it her father? Had Pete told him?

"Janie?" her mother called from the kitchen. "Phone for you. It's Bryan."

Not her father, but almost as bad. Bryan Manning had dated her a few times after she stopped seeing Pete. He had recently moved from Chicago and didn't know too many people.

He was a nice man, but she couldn't continue to see him.

"Hello, Bryan," she said, trying to make her voice cheerful.

"Hi, Janie. How's life?"

If he only knew.

"Um, fine, Bryan."

"How about dinner tomorrow night? We could grab a steak in town."

"I can't." She should explain, but how could she?

"Then Friday night? I've thought about you constantly. You're the best thing I've found since I left Chicago."

The warmth in his voice was touching, as well as his words. She'd give anything to hear that sentiment from Pete. In fact, everything about Bryan was great. He was handsome, successful, warm, loving—but he wasn't Pete.

"I can't go out with you anymore, Bryan," she finally managed to say.

After a tense silence, he asked in a low voice, "What did I do, Janie? Whatever it is, I'll change. You mean a lot to me. I can't—"

"Bryan! It's not you. It's me. I—I can't date for a while."

"Problem with your parents? You could move out. I'll gladly share my digs," he offered with a laugh he couldn't quite pull off.

Trying to inject some lightheartedness into her voice, she replied, "Thanks for the generosity, but I can't do that. After all, I work here."

More silence. "What is it, Janie? Is there anything I can do?"

Tenderness. Concern. His reaction was soothing, but she couldn't take advantage of him. Maybe she should just tell him the truth. After all, she would tell her father as soon as he returned, so it wouldn't hurt to tell Bryan now.

"No, there's nothing you can do. I—I'm pregnant, Bryan."

She expected him to retreat at once. Babies tended to scare bachelors.

"So you're getting married?" he asked instead.

"Um, no," she replied. "I really have to go, Bryan."

"Wait. Did the father refuse to marry you?"

"No."

"Then why aren't you getting married?"

"Bryan, you really shouldn't—"

"I'll marry you."

She was speechless.

After waiting for her to respond, Bryan plowed on. "Look, I know it's too soon to tell you, but I love you. I'll love your baby. I'll take care of the two of you."

"Bryan, please. This is impossible. You can't— This doesn't make sense."

"Yes, it does. Think about it, Janie."

The urgency in his voice convinced her he was serious. But she still couldn't consider his offer. "No, I'm sorry, Bryan."

"Look, can I at least call you? Take you out? I mean, if you're not marrying the man, then we can still see each other. Give me a chance, Janie."

"I'll—I'll think about it." That was all she could promise him. She just needed some time.

"Janie!"

Her father's roar drew her attention away from Bryan.

"I have to go now, Bryan."

He was still protesting as she hung up, but she couldn't spare any time for him at the moment. She had to face her father.

When she entered the kitchen, she discovered her mother and father facing each other, hands on their hips. *Oh, great. Not only is my life a mess, I'm going to ruin theirs, too.*

"She will too!" her father shouted.

"Hi, Dad."

Her greeting drew his immediate attention. He didn't waste any time making his position clear. "Young lady, I'm very unhappy with you. But you *will* marry Pete Randall. Make no mistake about it!"

"No, Daddy, I won't," she replied softly, refusing to join him in a shouting match.

He gaped at her, as if she'd never opposed him before, though they had had some spectacular arguments in the past. After all, she was her father's daughter.

"What did you say? Janie, you have to! You're going to have his baby."

"I know that, Daddy." She knew it better than anyone. "But I'm not going to marry Pete. He doesn't love me."

"He wants to marry you!" her father insisted.

"That's not the same thing."

"Hank," Lavinia interrupted before he could speak again, "Janie's tired. She doesn't need all this harassment."

"Harassment? What are you talking about, woman? I'm her father, in case you've forgotten! It's my duty to guide her. I know what's best for her, and she'll do what I say."

Lavinia stepped to Janie's side and put her arm around her. "No. She'll do what she thinks is right."

"Surely you're not on her side? Lavinia, what are you thinking about?"

"I'm thinking about Janie," Lavinia said quietly.

It wasn't often her parents disagreed. They were a wonderful couple, as loving now as when they'd married. But neither of them gave in easily, either.

"Now, Lavinia..." Hank began, eyeing his wife warily.

"No, Hank. I will not have you browbeating Janie. She's not at full strength right now."

Janie's heart filled as her father spun around to face her, panic and caring on his face. "You're not well? Is something wrong with the baby?" he hurriedly demanded.

"No, Daddy. I'm fine. Everything's fine."

"How dare you scare me to death!" he yelled, turning back to Lavinia.

"I was referring to her pregnancy, Hank. Surely, after all my difficulties, you know how delicate her condition is."

Janie's mother had miscarried twice before she'd given birth to Janie and once afterward. Then the doctor had ordered no more pregnancies.

One of Janie's hands stole to cover her stomach. Already this baby was so real that even the thought of losing it frightened her.

Her mother's words also affected her father. "Now, Lavinia, honey, you know I wouldn't do anything to upset Janie, but she has to marry Pete. Surely you can see that."

"No, she doesn't. She has to do what's best for her and the baby."

"That's what I said. She has to marry Pete."

"Daddy, I can't."

"Why not?" came a deep voice from the doorway.

"PETE!" JANIE GASPED.

"Sorry for not waiting for you to open the door, Lavinia," Pete apologized, but his gaze didn't leave Janie. He wanted her to tell him one more time why his child would be born a bastard. "I didn't think anyone was going to hear my knock."

"That's all right, Pete," Lavinia assured him.

To his relief, she offered him a gentle smile. Since his mother's death, Lavinia had watched over him and his brothers acting as surrogate mother on many occasions. He hadn't wanted her mad at him.

Now he turned his attention back to Janie. "Tell me again, Janie, why you won't marry me."

Her stubborn chin rose, and she looked away. "You know why."

"I want to be sure. I want to know why you're refusing to give my baby my name. I may have to explain it to him when he's older." He squared his shoulders and glared at her. He was a lot bigger and older than her. He wasn't averse to using intimidation if it meant she gave in.

He almost chuckled out loud as Janie reminded him that he was dreaming if he thought he could intimidate her.

"*You* won't have to explain anything to *my* baby." Her body language said he'd better think again if he thought he could take her down.

"*Our* baby will expect me to explain."

"Who said I was going to tell the baby who the daddy is?"

Pete's mouth dropped open. It had never occurred to him that his child might not know who he was. "*I'll* tell him, if you don't!"

"You're yelling, just like Daddy."

Pete cast a guilty look at Hank. He'd come because he'd known Hank wouldn't be able to persuade Janie. Not alone. He'd thought maybe the two of them could do the job. But now he looked for reinforcements. "Lavinia, talk some sense into her."

Before she could answer, Hank said, "She's on Janie's side. No use asking her for help."

"Lavinia?" Pete repeated, shocked by Hank's words. "Surely you understand that it will be best for Janie and the baby for her to marry me."

He held his breath as Lavinia considered her response. Finally, with an arm still around Janie, she said, "I'm afraid that has to be Janie's decision, Pete. I support whatever she decides to do." She looked at her daughter. "Perhaps you two should talk again without us old folks interfering."

Lavinia took Hank's arm and led him from the kitchen. Suddenly Pete found himself once again alone with Janie. What he said now might determine his child's future. He wet his lips and frantically sought for the right words.

"Pete," Janie whispered, speaking before he could. "Don't do this."

"What? Don't do what, Janie? Fight for the right to give my name to my son? To acknowledge him before everyone?"

"Why are you so sure it's a boy?" she demanded, turning her back on him.

He pulled her around to face him. "Boy, girl, it doesn't matter, Janie. What matters is this is my baby."

She stared at her toes, refusing to look at him. "I'm not denying the baby is yours, Pete."

"I don't see how you could!" he exclaimed. He knew the baby was his. But in the back of his thoughts was the man she'd been seeing. He didn't want any doubt at all in anyone's mind.

"I'll leave it up to you."

He frowned. What had he missed? "Leave what up to me?"

"It will be your choice as to whether or not you publicly claim to be the father."

He stared at her, totally lost by her words. "What are you talking about? Did you think I'd deny my own child?" His voice rose as outrage filled it.

"Not—not exactly but—"

"Damn it, Janie, I'll shout from the rooftop that this baby is mine! And don't you forget it!"

"You're yelling again," she protested, her gaze lifting to his.

"Damn right I'm yelling! You're driving me crazy!"

The stubborn look on her face, her eyes sparking with challenge, took his breath away. The fire in her always lit a corresponding one in him, one that quickly burned out of control.

Groaning, he pulled her into his embrace. "Aw, Janie," he crooned, his body shuddering as her softness went all the way through him. He tilted her chin, his lips descended to hers and he drank from the sweetest fountain in the world. He never wanted to let her go, to let her put the distance between them that had driven him crazy the past three weeks.

Her arms stole around his neck, and he pressed her even closer, wanting her to feel his arousal, to know that she made him ache with need. From the very beginning, she'd had that effect on him.

"I knew it! I knew Pete would talk her into it!" Hank shouted from the kitchen door.

Chapter Three

Her father's words ripped Janie from Pete's embrace. She was grateful for the intervention. Once again, she'd proved to herself how easily Pete could erase all her carefully constructed barriers.

"No! No, Daddy. Pete hasn't convinced me." She drew a deep breath and pasted that practiced smile on her face. "He was just...assuring me of his support." She couldn't quite bring herself to meet Pete's gaze, but she heard his snort of derision.

"That so, Pete?" Hank asked.

"Yeah, right," Pete said, but the tone of his voice didn't match the agreement in his words.

"Well, it seems to me that you shouldn't be kissing like that unless you're going to get married," Hank said, a frown on his face.

"Daddy! You're being ridiculous." Janie risked a quick glance at Pete and discovered his cheeks were as red as hers felt. As if they hadn't done a lot more. Otherwise, she wouldn't be pregnant.

"Hank," Lavinia said quietly.

"You know I'm right, Lavinia. They shouldn't be carrying on like that."

"I think that's what my father said when we told him I was pregnant," Lavinia said calmly, staring at her husband.

Hank's face reddened and he tried to speak several times. Finally he muttered, "I can't believe you said that."

"It's true."

"You mean you were pregnant when you and Daddy got married?" Janie blurted out, staring at her parents.

"I refuse to discuss this subject!" Hank roared, looking anywhere but at Janie or her mother.

"But, Daddy—"

"Whatever happened, your mother and I got married! Can you match that, young lady?"

Janie gave her father a rueful smile. "No," she said, shaking her head. "I can't. You see, you and Mom loved each other and—and that's not the case with us."

"Janie—" Pete began, but halted as someone knocked on the back door.

"Who could that be?" Lavinia wondered aloud as she hurried to open it.

"Good afternoon, Mrs. Dawson," Bryan Manning said, but his gaze flew over her shoulder, seeking out Janie. "May I speak to your daughter?"

Janie closed her eyes. Just what she needed. Another determined male wanting to make choices for her. She opened her eyes and stepped forward. "Bryan, this really isn't a good time."

"But it can't wait, Janie. I want to tell your dad that I'm the father of your baby. We can be married at once." He smiled at her, reminding her of a little boy expecting to be rewarded.

Instead, she wanted to bash him on the head.

Before she could protest, the other three in the kitchen burst into questions. The babble of voices made her cover her ears.

Pete immediately seized her wrists and pulled her hands away as he leaned down to face her, nose to nose. "What the hell is he talking about?"

"Take your hands off her," Bryan protested, advancing on Pete.

"Back off, greenhorn, before you find yourself flat on your back," Pete growled, turning to face him.

Janie immediately inserted herself between the two men. "Pete, don't start anything."

"You're warning *me*?" Pete demanded, his voice rising in protest. "I'm not the one who's sticking his nose in where it doesn't belong." He glared at Bryan.

Janie ignored Pete. Bryan was the problem, and she wanted him gone as soon as possible. "Bryan, what are you doing here? I said I'd think about it."

"You'd think about what?" Pete demanded, even more outrage in his voice.

"Yeah, just what have you been planning with this man?" Hank chipped in.

"You really should explain, dear," Lavinia added.

"And how did he know about my baby?" Pete demanded. "Is that why you refused to marry me? You already were making plans with *him*?"

Bryan tensed even more and surged toward Pete in response to the scorn in his voice.

"No!" Janie yelled, extending her arms straight out between the two men. It had always looked so romantic in the movies when two men fought over a woman. In reality, it wasn't romantic—it was chaotic!

She drew a deep breath. "If you would give me a moment alone with Bryan, I'd appreciate it."

"You haven't answered our questions," her father reminded her.

"No, Daddy, I haven't. But I'd prefer to do that after I've explained things to Bryan. If you don't mind."

Even as her father opened his mouth—to protest, she assumed—Pete spoke up. "I don't think you should be left alone with him."

Janie gave a sigh of exasperation. "Right. He's certainly dangerous, isn't he? Come on, Pete, we're not dealing with a mass murderer here. Bryan is a friend. He made his offer out of—of friendship." She couldn't help sending a look of apology to Bryan. After all, she didn't mean to trivialize his feelings, but she *wanted* what they shared to be friendship.

Pete was watching her closely and settled his hands on his hips, his mouth tightening. Finally he said, "All right, I'll give you five minutes."

Janie's patience fled. A few minutes ago, she'd been in heaven in Pete's arms. But that didn't give him the right to lay down the law to her. "Listen, mister," she said, poking him in the chest with her forefinger, "I'll take all the time I need. And if you get tired of waiting, feel free to head on home."

She was quite pleased with herself, finally feeling she'd gained control of the situation. But her stomach quickly erased her superiority. She barely made it to the sink before she threw up her lunch.

LAVINIA TOOK CHARGE, shooing the men away from Janie. "I'll take care of her," she said, leading Janie out of the kitchen. "She'll be just fine." Just before they disappeared, she added in a stern voice, "And we want no fighting down here."

As soon as the door closed behind the two women, Bryan spoke. "Look, Mr. Dawson, I love your daughter. I'll take care of her, if she'll marry me. And the baby, too."

Pete didn't wait for Hank to respond. He was too afraid. "The baby is mine, and I've already offered marriage to Janie. *I* will take care of both of them."

"When I talked to Janie, she said she wasn't marrying you," Bryan challenged.

"Things change. Janie will marry me." He only hoped he was right. But he wasn't going to show his fears to this man.

"Well, until Janie tells me differently, I'll be here, ready to take care of her."

"She doesn't need you," Pete growled, irritated that the man didn't recognize that he was treading on Pete's territory. It had torn him up that Janie was out with another man the past three weeks. That the man claimed to love her made him want to punch something...or someone.

Hank spoke up. "Boy, if you've got a lick of sense in your head, you'll say your goodbyes now. Pete's a little riled up as it is, and I'm worried about my little girl.''

''But I want to talk to Janie,'' the man insisted.

Pete shook his head. This guy wasn't right for Janie. Why couldn't she see that? He flexed his hands, itching to show Bryan the door a little forcefully.

''You're not bothering Janie now. Just go,'' Hank insisted, and Pete nodded in agreement.

''Why does he get to stay?'' Bryan pointed to Pete, just in case Hank didn't understand whom he meant.

'' 'Cause I want him to, and it's my house,'' Hank replied, his voice growing louder.

Both Pete and Hank took a step closer to Bryan, and he began backing toward the door. ''Okay, okay, I'm going. But I'll be back. I won't abandon Janie.''

As the door closed behind him, Pete and Hank looked at each other with relief.

''Son, I don't mind telling you, I'd much rather have you married to Janie than that Easterner.''

''I'd get a big head about that statement, Hank, except that I don't think Bryan is much competition,'' Pete drawled, still scowling at the door.

''Maybe not, but at least he's willing to say the words Janie wants to hear.'' Hank gave Pete a steady look. ''You may find him more competition than you think.''

Pete refused to even consider such a thing. Janie was having *his* baby. He couldn't believe she wouldn't listen to him eventually. Then he turned his thoughts to a more important matter. ''What about Janie? Is she all right?''

"Yeah, or Lavinia would've already been on the phone calling Doc. You'd better get used to her throwing up. Lavinia always did."

Pete shook his head. No question about it. The female was the stronger of the two sexes. He didn't think he could stand throwing up very often.

The kitchen door opened, and both men snapped to attention when Lavinia walked in.

"How's Janie?" Pete asked.

"She's fine. I've got her lying down. Don't we have some club soda around here, Hank?"

Her husband hurried to the pantry, and she turned to Pete. "Did Bryan leave?"

"Yeah, with a little encouragement."

"You two didn't come to blows, did you? Janie was worried about that."

"Of course not. I behaved myself." He ignored Hank's chuckle. "Can I see Janie?"

Hand returned with a bottle of club soda. "Better not, son. She's in no mood to be talked to now."

"I think it will be all right," Lavinia contradicted, but she gave Pete a warning look. "As long as you don't upset her. It was all that arguing and stress that caused her to throw up. It's not good for the baby."

"Lavinia, I don't think it's a good idea," Hank said, frowning.

She turned to stare at her husband with that determined look that Pete had seen a thousand times, and he grinned at the older man. "I know who's going to win this argument, because I've seen that look on your daughter's face. You two can discuss it in private while I visit with Janie." He turned to go to the door and then added at the last minute, "I promise I won't upset her."

He knew the way to Janie's room, though he hadn't been there in a number of years, not since the summer he'd helped Hank paint the upstairs for some extra spending money. He rapped on her door and heard her faint permission to enter.

"Hi, Janie," he said quietly, his gaze roaming her pale face.

"Pete! I—I was afraid it was Bryan."

Her word choice did a lot for his morale. "Nope. We told him to leave." Immediately he held up his hand. "Nicely, we told him nicely." He grinned and sighed with relief when she grinned back.

"Yeah, I bet."

He crossed over to the bed and sat down on the edge of it. "I was as nice as I could be."

She raised her eyebrows. "That might not be saying too much."

He smiled at her but turned the conversation to her health. "How are you? Still feeling bad?"

She sobered and shook her head. "No. Just a little tired. It's been a—a busy day."

"I'll say." He reached over and took her hand. "I'm not going to argue with you anymore. I promised your mother. But I wanted to be sure you're all right, you and the baby, before I left."

Pete didn't know what he'd said wrong, but the darkening of Janie's blue eyes before she lowered her lashes told him he'd upset her. He tightened his grasp on her hand. "Is everything all right?"

"Everything's fine."

"So why won't you look at me?"

His question brought her gaze back to him, a challenge in those blue eyes. He'd known she'd respond to a dare. She always had. Once she'd broken her arm because Chad had dared her to jump out of a tree. Both of them had caught hell from Hank and Lavinia.

Without conscious thought, he leaned over and brushed her lips with his. "I wanted you to know I'm not going away. I'm not giving up. We're going to be married, Janie Dawson, and you might as well resign yourself to that fact. Okay?"

She tugged on her hand. "No, it's not okay. We've been through this already."

He held on, not wanting to break contact with her. "I'm not going to argue with you right now. Just think about what I've said."

"And you think about what I've said," she said, her chin rising.

"That's my Janie," Pete said, his grin returning. "Never give in."

"I was afraid you'd forgotten," she returned.

"Nope." His voice grew serious. "I've never forgotten anything about you, Janie, and I'm not likely to." He kissed her again and stood. "Don't you forget that, either."

Then he walked away, fighting the desire to crawl into bed with her and cuddle her against him, protecting and loving—no, caring for her. That's right. Caring for her. He didn't love Janie, of course. But he cared about her.

He just had to convince her that caring was good enough.

JAMIE STARED at the ceiling, biting her bottom lip to stall the tears that pooled in her eyes. Was she being stubborn for the sake of stubbornness? Should she give in to Pete's determination?

With a sniff of her nose, she answered those questions. No, she wanted the best for her baby...and for her. Pete would be a good daddy. But she wanted a husband, too. Someone like her father, who loved his wife more than anything.

She'd never doubted her father's love for her, his only daughter, but she had always known that he loved her mother even more. And that was as it should be.

When Pete loved her, not just their baby, then she'd accept marriage with him. Until then, she'd hold out. Even if it meant being alone.

"WHERE'D YOU GO?" Jake asked when Pete appeared in the big barn housing the indoor arena where they worked their animals away from the harsh Wyoming winter.

"I followed Hank back to his place. I figured he'd need help with Janie." He pulled his Stetson down farther over his eyes, hoping his brother wouldn't read the turmoil he knew was there.

"And?"

"And what?"

"Are we going to have a wedding?"

Pete looked anywhere but at Jake. He loved his brother, but he was going to have to disappoint him. "Not yet."

"So what are you going to do?"

"I don't know."

"Pete, you only have a few more months. Don't you think you ought to make some plans?"

He whirled around to stare at Jake. "I'm trying to figure out what to do. But you know how stubborn Janie can be."

Jake nodded. "We'll think on it together. There's got to be some way."

"Some way for what?" a throaty feminine voice asked behind them.

Both men spun around to face B. J. Anderson, the new veterinarian to the area. She and her aunt and four-year-old son lived in a house on the Randall ranch. Though she'd only been there a week or two, already she was fitting in well.

"Hi, B.J." Pete said, forcing a smile in greeting.

Jake simply nodded.

"Is there a problem I can help with?"

"Nope," Jake said emphatically.

B.J. didn't seem to take offense at his blunt dismissal of her offer, but Pete had another reason for apologizing.

"Don't mind Jake. He's not used to being around females."

"That's all right. I didn't intend to stick my nose in where it's not wanted."

"Well, actually I might ask you a question or two, if you don't mind. I mean, you being a female and all." Pete watched her carefully to see if she would mind offering advice.

Though her gaze fell first on Jake, as if to determine whether he would forbid any exchanges, she smiled at Pete. "Well, I'm definitely female, so ask away."

Now that he had someone to advise him, Pete didn't know exactly how to begin. He looked helplessly at Jake.

"Don't expect me to lead this discussion. It wasn't my idea to drag a stranger into it." Jake glared at B.J.

Pete saw B.J. stiffen, and he figured she'd walk away, but instead her chin rose just slightly and she turned a little more pointedly toward Pete. It reminded him of Janie's stubbornness.

"What's the problem? Something to do with a female?" B.J. asked encouragingly. "You have a cow with a problem?"

"No! No, it's not about a cow. It's not professional. I mean, for a vet. I—I'm going to be a daddy."

Though B.J. was momentarily stunned by his words, she quickly offered her congratulations. "That's wonderful, Pete. When's the wedding?"

Jake snorted, and B.J. looked at him in surprise. "Did I say something funny?"

"You could say that," Jake drawled.

"That's the problem," Pete hurriedly said. "She won't agree to marry me."

B.J. tilted her head to one side, as if seeing him for the first time. "Did you ask her?"

"Of course I did. She—she said no."

"Is there someone else she's going to marry? I haven't seen you dating anyone since I've been here, so—"

"No! She's not going to marry anyone else!" When Pete realized he was shouting, he drew a deep breath before explaining, "She's been seeing someone else, but the baby is *mine.*"

"She's not still seeing him?" Jake asked quickly, a frown on his face.

"I don't know. He showed up today and—and he proposed marriage. Told Hank the baby was his," Pete hissed, anger filling his voice.

"Oh, my," B.J. said with a sigh. "Wyoming is a lot more interesting than my old stomping grounds in Kansas City. This sounds like a plot line on one of the soaps my aunt watches."

"So tell me what to do," Pete ordered.

B.J. looked first at Pete and then Jake. "About what?"

"How do I get her to marry me? I've told her she's going to, but Janie's as stubborn as a mule."

B.J.'s lips curved into a slow smile. "You *told* her she was going to marry you?"

"Yeah. And she is." Pete had to keep believing his words because if he didn't, he'd go crazy.

B.J. chuckled. "Pete, haven't you ever heard you catch more bears with honey?"

"What do you mean?"

"She means," Jake began, his voice laden with sarcasm, "you should waltz around Janie with flowers and candy in your hands."

B.J. shot a cool look at Jake before she spoke. "Flowers and candy are a start. But a woman agrees to marry a man when she believes that she matters to him more than any other woman in the world. Have you convinced her you love her?"

Pete's face turned red, and he looked away. Jake moved closer to his brother and muttered, "That's a useless emotion."

B.J. appeared even more stunned by that pronouncement than by Pete's imminent fatherhood. "I beg your pardon?"

"Look, B.J.," Pete said, desperate to explain things before Jake exploded. "Our experiences with females have left the Randall brothers a little scarred. I told Janie I'd take care of her and the baby. That's all she needs to know."

B.J. gave both of them a considering look that had Pete squirming before she smiled at him. "Then, Pete, I'm afraid you'll have a hard time convincing Janie to marry you. Women don't want to be taken care of—they want emotional commitment."

Pete didn't like the way this conversation was going.

"The woman isn't the only one who wants commitment," Jake intervened, his voice harsh with emotion.

Pete knew his brother was thinking of his own failed marriage. They had all suffered through the breakup. Since Chloe, Jake's ex-wife, had been the first female on the ranch since their mother's death at Chad's birth, twenty-six years ago, their exposure to life with a female had been an unhappy one.

To Pete's surprise, B.J. smiled at Jake. "Once bitten, twice shy?"

"You're damn right," Jake returned, for once appearing to agree with the vet.

"Well, then, boys, I have one bit of advice for you—you'd better get your snake-bite kit ready, because Pete here is going to have to stick his neck out if he's going to convince his woman to marry him." With a smile and a wave of her hand, she strode out of the barn.

Chapter Four

Lavinia insisted Janie take it easy the next day. After the high drama she'd experienced, Janie didn't argue. It was a relief to wake up without losing her breakfast. That was a start in the right direction.

She spent most of the day in her father's office. Though she participated in the actual running of the ranch, she also did a lot of the paperwork, using her computer skills to update the files.

After college, she'd considered moving to Casper to find a job, but her father had offered her a paid position with him. After all, he'd pointed out, it was her heritage. Who better to help him?

She'd agreed. Her heart was on the ranch. She loved the life-style. And it had kept her close to Pete Randall. That thought brought a big sigh.

"Janie?" Lavinia called just before she appeared in the doorway. "There's a flower delivery for you."

Janie was surprised. The florist in the nearest town charged a fortune to deliver to the ranches, so the thrifty ranchers seldom bothered with that city tradition.

To her astonishment, she had two deliveries, both huge floral arrangements. The deliveryman was waiting in the kitchen, the flowers on the table, a huge grin on his face.

"Hi, Buddy." She'd gone to high school with him.

"Hi, Janie. Looks like you got yourself two beaux."

She gave him the cash she'd pulled out of a desk drawer for a tip before she came to the kitchen and thanked him, not anxious to add to the rumors that would be flying around the countryside.

"Aren't you gonna open the notes before I go?" Buddy asked, lingering.

"Nope."

"Want to know who they're from?" he asked hopefully.

"Nope. But thanks for bringing them, Buddy," she added pointedly, walking him to the door.

"No problem. Thanks for the tip."

She waited at the door until she saw his truck drive away before turning to face her equally curious mother. "I guess I have no excuse to avoid reading those notes now. If those two put anything in them that will cause more rumors, I'll kill them both!"

"Maybe they're not from those two boys chasing after you. Could be from—from a business acquaintance," Lavinia offered, a smile on her face.

"Yeah, sure." Janie unpinned the first envelope and read it.

Dear Janie,
I wanted roses, but the florist said she didn't have

any. But these flowers are to assure you of my
love. Think about my offer.

> Love, Bryan

With a groan, she put the note down and unpinned the second.

Janie,
Don't forget what I said.

> Pete

Hysterical laughter bubbled up inside her. How
typical of the two men. Both had been discreet. But
what a difference.

"Well? Are they from Pete and Bryan?" Lavinia
asked.

"Of course," she acknowledged with a sigh.

"Thoughtful."

"Mmm. Yes, but sure to cause a lot of talk. When
I start showing in a few weeks, everyone is going to
remember these flowers, and gossip will spread all
over the county."

"Honey," Lavinia said, a rueful smile on her face,
"when you start showing with no wedding ring on
your finger, gossip is going to run rampant, flowers
or no flowers."

"I know. Are you sure you don't want me to go
away, Mom?"

Lavinia crossed the kitchen and wrapped her arms
around her daughter. "No, I don't want you to go

away. A little gossip is not going to splinter our family."

"Thanks, Mom," Janie whispered, hugging her tightly in return. "I think I'll go finish my work."

Two hours later, her mother again summoned her to the kitchen, where she found a grinning Mr. Jones. Ever since she could remember, as a child she'd visited his store, a modern-day general store, in Rawhide, clutching her allowance in her hands, eager to spend it on his motley collection of merchandise.

"Mr. Jones! How nice to see you," she greeted him with a smile, but behind that smile was a search for the reason for his visit.

"Howdy, Janie. Nice to see you, too. But I'm here on business."

"Business?"

Instead of answering, he nodded toward the kitchen table. For the first time, Janie noticed the two packages on the table, each with its own huge bow.

"What are those?" she asked, dread building in her.

"Gifts, with special delivery instructions. The biggest boxes of chocolate I had."

She assumed his broad smile meant the fees for special delivery had been handsome, in addition to his finally unloading merchandise that had lingered on the shelf too long. "I see. Well, thanks for making the delivery."

Her mother handed her some bills for a tip, but when she offered them to Mr. Jones, he refused. "No, no, that's not necessary. They paid me well. Enjoy the chocolates," he added before leaving.

Janie looked at her mother and sighed. "This is ridiculous."

"Yes, it is, but I suspect it's also amusing the entire community. It will take you a while to live this courting down."

"It will take a while to eat all those chocolates, too. And if I do, I'll have a new nickname, 'the Blob.'"

"Well, open them up. I feel like a chocolate break," Lavinia said, and poured them each a cup of coffee.

When Hank came in half an hour later, he found both the females of his family sitting at the kitchen table surrounded by their bounty. "What's going on?"

"Have a piece of candy, Daddy," Janie offered.

"What's the occasion?"

"Your daughter is being courted by her two suitors." Lavinia picked up another piece of chocolate. "And I'm enjoying it."

"Damn! What's wrong with those boys?" Hank fumed. "Don't they know it'll cause a lot of talk?"

"Oh, Hank, just sit down and have some chocolate."

Hank followed his wife's suggestion. But he suddenly wondered if he should've sent Lavinia chocolates every once in a while. She sure seemed to be enjoying Janie's.

WHAT DID HE DO NOW? Pete asked himself. He had sent flowers and chocolates yesterday. When he'd called last night, he talked to Hank, but Janie had refused to speak to him. Seemed like his gifts didn't help any.

What else could he send her?

What else could he do?

"Well?" Jake asked, walking up beside him.

"Well what?"

"Did you send the flowers?"

"Yeah, and candy, too."

Brett paused beside them, cocking one eyebrow. "Kind of expensive, isn't it?"

"Yeah, but Janie's worth it. Only, she wouldn't even talk to me on the phone last night." Pete frowned at the cowboys on the cutting horses in the arena as if it were their fault.

"Not a good sign," Brett said calmly.

Why not be calm? His future wasn't at stake, Pete thought glumly.

"Now what?" Jake asked.

"I don't know. I can't figure out what to do."

"Maybe something a little more personal. Anyone can order flowers," Brett stated.

"Anyone with a lot of money," Jake added.

"Manning sent her flowers and candy, too." Pete wasn't sure how much money the man had, but he seemed as determined as Pete in his pursuit of Janie.

One of the cowboys called from across the arena. "Pete? Telephone."

Jake had had phones put in all the barns several years ago. It saved them a lot of steps. Pete figured one of the rodeos he'd been in contact with had a question about the animals he was going to supply.

"Hello?"

"Pete, it's Hank. I figured you might like to know that Lavinia sent Janie into town to do some grocery shopping. If she won't talk to you on the phone, she can't refuse to speak to you over broccoli."

"Okay, I'll track her down there. Thanks, Hank." Whether it was in produce or dairy, she'd talk to him, all right.

JANIE NAVIGATED the streets of Rawhide with reluctance. She hadn't wanted to come to town so soon after the flowers and candy. But her mother needed some things right away. Besides, the weatherman said another snowstorm was moving in. It didn't pay to be short of supplies during the winter.

At least it was the middle of the day, when most people would be at work. She pulled into the almost-empty parking lot at the only grocery store in town.

Inside the store, she unbuttoned her coat, the sudden blast of heat thawing her out quickly.

"Hi, Janie," one of the checkers, Elizabeth Munger, called. Janie had gone to school with her, too. "Buddy said you've been getting some special deliveries."

Janie smiled and waved but kept on going. She hoped if she ignored those gifts, everyone would forget about them sooner. Pulling her mother's list out of her coat pocket, she began pushing the grocery cart up one aisle and down another, piling supplies in her cart.

"Hi, Janie. Figured you or your mother would be here," an older woman said. She was the wife of the rancher on the other side, opposite the Randalls.

"Hi, Mrs. Fisher. Stocking up?"

"You bet. When one of those storms hit, you know the menfolks will tend to the cows first and the roads last. Don't want to be caught short of the necessities...like chocolates." A big grin accompanied her teasing.

Janie smiled back, but she started pushing her cart again.

"Well, if that ain't a coincidence," Mrs. Fisher exclaimed, drawing Janie's attention. The woman was staring over Janie's shoulder, and she couldn't resist turning around.

"Hi, Janie, Mrs. Fisher," Pete said. "I just came into town to pick up a few things for Red."

"Really?" Mrs. Fisher said, her eyebrows soaring. "I thought Red always did his shopping on Mondays."

"He forgot some things."

Janie decided escape was the best plan while Pete was still talking to Mrs. Fisher. She resumed pushing her cart only to have one of Pete's big hands grab hold of the push bar.

"See you around, Mrs. Fisher," he said with a nod before turning to Janie.

"Turn loose of my cart," she whispered. To her surprise, he did as she asked, but he strolled along beside her.

"Why won't you talk to me, Janie?" he asked.

"We have nothing to talk about."

"You haven't thanked me for the candy and flowers."

"Oh, yes. How could I forget? Half the town has reminded me. Do you think they will have forgotten by the time I'm in maternity clothes?"

"Why the hell do I care? Do you still think I don't want to be known as the baby's father?"

"Shh!" It felt as if everyone in the store was following their progress, staring at them.

"Janie, what can I do to convince you—?"

"Hi, Janie."

They both whirled around. Janie recognized her second suitor's voice with a sinking heart.

"Hi, Bryan." She paused, sent an apologetic look to Pete and added, "Thanks for the candy and flowers."

Bryan beamed, and she could feel Pete tense beside her.

"I wanted you to remember what I said."

"I wouldn't forget. Now, if you'll excuse me, I have to finish shopping before the snowstorm arrives."

"Is it going to snow again? What's on the ground hasn't melted yet."

Pete snorted. "Well, it is Wyoming. If you don't like snow, come back in late spring."

Again Janie moved her cart, stopped and reached around Pete to pick up a large jar of peanut butter, her father's favorite late-night snack.

"Here, I'll get it for you," Bryan hurriedly said, and almost bumped heads with her to pick up her choice.

She drew back with a smothered sigh. "Thanks, Bryan, but really, I can manage."

"I like doing things for you," he assured her, an eager grin on his face.

Pete, beside her, scowled at the man before asking Janie, "What's next on your list?"

"Mother wants some cans of baked beans," Janie finally said. She sent him a look that said *Please back off*. But she knew he wouldn't. Not with Bryan hovering at her side.

For the next few minutes, they toured the grocery store, each man dashing from one side to the other to gather the groceries on Lavinia's list. All over the store, the other customers watched, gathering in twos and threes and whispering, big grins on their faces.

Janie felt as though she were leading the Fourth of July Parade. Only it was winter, they were in a grocery store, and there were only three of them. And she wished she wasn't one of the three.

Finally she reached the checkout stand. "Really, it was nice of you to help, but that's all my shopping."

"How about a cup of coffee?" Bryan asked.

"Sorry, the storm, you know."

"I'll follow you home to be sure you make it all right," Pete offered, but the caring that remark might have evoked was erased by the one-upmanship glare he sent Bryan's way.

"I could follow her home."

"No, Bryan, but thanks for the offer. You might have trouble getting back," Janie hastily said. The thought of Bryan having to stay at her house during a snowstorm was more than she could take.

During their discussion, Elizabeth, her old high-school friend, had been checking her out, ringing up each item and then staring at the three of them. Janie thought it must be the slowest checkout in history. The package boy, bagging the groceries, had to wait on the checker several times.

When Elizabeth pushed the empty cart past her toward the package boy, both men jumped into action, each grabbing a bag of groceries and stowing it in the cart. When the seven sacks were in place, Pete won the tussle over the cart.

Bryan immediately took advantage by taking Janie's arm. "I'll help you to your truck."

She couldn't meet Pete's hostile gaze. They both knew she didn't need any help getting to her truck. But she acquiesced to Bryan's offer, allowing him to draw her hand through his arm.

When they reached the truck, she pulled away from Bryan, who'd been filling her ears with compliments, to open the back of the vehicle.

Pete immediately began putting the paper bags in the truck, and Bryan joined in. As if they were in a race, they each grabbed a sack and then immediately wheeled around to grab the next. When there was only one sack left, she should've known what would happen next.

"I'll get it," Pete announced as he reached for the last sack.

"No, I'll get it!" Bryan said, trying to reach over Pete's strong arms. He managed to grasp a corner of the bag and pulled it in his direction. Pete, of course, had no intention of surrendering his hold. The rip of the paper announced the latest disaster.

Suddenly, canned goods were rolling across the parking lot. Potatoes landed with a plop in the unmelted mounds of snow surrounding the truck. The lettuce rolled over several times before coming to rest against the muddy tire of another vehicle.

She heard the laughter of those watching from the grocery store and covered her eyes. With both men apologizing, she picked up her groceries with a sigh. They weren't a parade. They were a freak show.

The package boy came out to help them retrieve the groceries, along with several other people in the parking lot. Mortified, Janie took their offerings with thanks and shoved them into the truck.

"Do you want me to go back in and get some more lettuce and potatoes? These got kind of dirty," Pete said.

"No, they'll wash. Just put them in the truck. They'll be fine." Anything to get out of there.

"I'm sorry," Bryan said again.

"It was an accident. And I appreciate your help." She paused and then shot a look at Pete, glowering beside her. "And yours, too, Pete."

"Yeah, I bet," Pete muttered, surveying their audience, still in place. "We made a spectacle of ourselves."

"Yeah, we were more exciting than the coming storm," she teased, breaking into a grin. It wasn't often she saw Pete Randall feeling sheepish. It was almost worth the embarrassment.

When he caught her smile, he returned it, and her spirits brightened. The man could bring sunshine to the gloomiest day ever. At least, he could for her.

"Come on. You'd better be on your way. I'll be right behind you."

She nodded and turned to tell Bryan goodbye.

"When will I see you?"

"I don't know. I'll—I'll call you in a few days."

Pete stiffened beside her, losing his endearing grin.

Bryan leaned toward her as if he would kiss her goodbye, but Janie ducked away. When they'd dated, she'd allowed him to kiss her good-night, but nothing more. And she had to admit that she hadn't particularly liked his kisses. She'd told herself to give their relationship time, but she had felt more than a hint of relief when the baby gave her a reason to stop seeing Bryan.

Now she had to tell him that.

But not today. She'd been through enough today. And she couldn't tell him the truth in front of Pete and all the other citizens of Rawhide who'd been drawn to the little trio's shopping trip.

All the way home, the sight of Pete in her rearview mirror was both a comfort and an ache. He'd always looked out for her, even when they'd been lovers. She corrected herself. Especially when they'd been lovers. He hadn't let anyone know about them because he was protecting her reputation, he'd said.

Well, everyone knew about them now. The candy, the flowers, the grocery shopping. She chuckled. From this distance, the grocery shopping was hysterical. But if the two men ever approached her again at the same time, she was going to run.

Reaching the turnoff to her house, she waved her hand in the back window to say thank you to Pete and braked for the turn. After she straightened out on the driveway, she checked her mirror, expecting to see Pete sail past her toward the Randall ranch.

Instead, he turned in after her.

Now what was he up to? Why was he following her?

She nibbled on her bottom lip, anxiety rising. In the grocery store, he couldn't bring up anything personal with everyone around. But here, at her house, she knew he could get her alone.

With a sigh, she parked the truck. By the time she got to the back of the vehicle to open it, Pete was beside her.

"What are you doing here? Don't you need to get home before the storm?"

"The radio said it might hold off for a day or two," he said, and reached past her for a grocery sack.

"I can carry the groceries in, Pete," she protested.

"I don't think pregnant ladies are supposed to carry anything heavy."

She heaved a big sigh. "I'm not an invalid."

As she reached for a grocery sack herself, Pete ordered, "Leave it, Janie, and go inside."

"Pete Randall, stop ordering me around!"

"Janie Dawson, use your head. There's no point in taking risks. And if you're good, I'll take the blame for the spilled groceries."

She stared at him, her mouth dropping open. Then

she sputtered, "You'll take the blame? Like it's not really your fault?"

"That's right." He swooped down and kissed her before reaching for a second sack. "I figure it's your fault for flirting with that greenhorn. But I'll forgive you," he said magnanimously, a twinkle in his eye. "Now get inside."

Chapter Five

Pete figured he had a big advantage over Bryan Manning. Lavinia liked him. He hoped to parlay that liking into an invitation to dine with the Dawsons.

"Howdy, Lavinia," he greeted her with a smile when he entered the kitchen with the first bags of groceries. Janie was standing beside the door, her arms crossed and her foot tapping.

"Well, hi Pete. What are you doing here?"

"Helping Janie with the groceries. I was worried about her lifting anything heavy."

Lavinia looked first at her daughter and then back to Pete. "That's real thoughtful of you, Pete. But why does Janie look so irritated?"

Pete cleared his throat. "Well, it could have something to do with one of the grocery sacks splitting. I think she's worried about the lettuce."

"I don't think so," Janie retorted, one eyebrow raised. At her mother's questioning look, she continued, "You should have seen the two of them, Mom."

"Two? I only see one." Lavinia pretended to peer around Pete for another person.

"Bryan showed up at the grocery store, too. And they created a spectacle."

Lavinia looked at Pete. "Should I hope the grocery store was empty?"

"'Fraid not, Lavinia. But I tried to be discreet."

"You wouldn't know the meaning of the word if it slapped you in the face," returned Janie, but Pete was relieved to see a twinkle in her eye.

"I bet you never finished your shopping that fast." His broad grin won an answering smile.

"No, I suppose not. I was so embarrassed I would've run up and down the aisles if I could have."

"What did those two do?" Lavinia asked.

"They turned my shopping into a competition, dashing around, each one trying to fill the cart before the other one could. They almost turned old Mrs. Capelli upside down with their mad rush."

"That's not true," Pete protested. "We only turned her around a time or two. And I helped her find the canned tuna." His righteous tone brought a laugh from Lavinia.

"A true act of charity, Pete. Are you going to bring in the rest of the groceries before they freeze, by the way?"

"Yes, ma'am!" he said, snapping a salute and sailing out the door. At least he'd mentioned the torn sack without Lavinia being irritated. When he returned two minutes later, with two more bags, Lavinia was leaning against the sink, laughing.

"What have you been telling her?" he asked Janie suspiciously.

"I was just describing your expertise at putting the groceries *in* the truck."

The flash of Janie's eyes, accompanied by a broad smile, reminded him of happier times. The urge to pull her into his arms and kiss her until she melted against him almost overcame him. But the knowledge that she would resist made him hold back.

That and Lavinia's presence.

He headed back out for the other groceries. When he set these sacks on the counter, Lavinia fulfilled his hopes.

"You'll stay for dinner, Pete? It's the least we can do for your helping Janie at the grocery store."

"I'd love to stay, Lavinia, on one condition."

"And that is . . . ?"

"You have to promise not to let Janie near the food before I eat," Pete said deadpan. "She's sure to poison my share if she gets the chance."

"LAVINIA," PETE SAID with a sigh, "don't you tell Red I said so, but you must be the best cook in the whole state of Wyoming."

"Thank you, Pete, but I can't take all the credit. Janie made the apple pie."

Janie wanted to stick out her tongue at Pete and assure him she hadn't made it for him. Instead, she received his praises with a nod of her head. But she lost her calm with his next remark.

"You don't have to convince me Janie would make a good wife, Lavinia. I know that already. She's the one who's being stubborn. Maybe someone should be praising *me* to the skies to change *her* mind."

"Maybe *someone* should accept the answer he's already gotten!" Janie snapped.

"Janie!" Hank protested.

More effective than her father's protest was Lavinia's steady regard. Dinner had been fun, like old times, and Janie immediately regretted losing her temper. Especially when she knew she'd disappointed her mother.

"Sorry," she apologized with a small smile.

Pete leaned across the table toward her. "My fault. I shouldn't have brought up such a personal topic here at the table."

"I don't see why not, Pete. It concerns all of us," Hank asserted, his chin jutting out in stubbornness.

"It may concern us, Hank, but the decision has to be Pete and Janie's." Lavinia stood. "Just to show you how generous I am, Pete, I'm going to let you and Janie do the dishes, which should give you half an hour alone. Then Janie might want you to leave so she can get some rest."

When Hank didn't move, instead staring at his wife in surprise, she prodded him. "Come on, Hank. These young people want to be alone."

"Thanks, Lavinia," Pete murmured as Janie's parents left the room.

Janie, on the other hand, promised herself to have a talk with her mother tomorrow. Lavinia *knew* her daughter didn't want to be alone with Pete.

Janie got to her feet. "I'll rinse and load the dishwasher. You clear the table."

"Let's talk first," Pete suggested.

"Oh, no. One or both of us will get upset, and you'll leave and I'll be stuck with all the work. You're not getting out of it that easy, Pete Randall."

"Well, I thought I'd give it a try," he said with a grin, and began stacking the dishes to bring them to the sink.

They worked in silence for several minutes. Janie was determined to leave any talking to Pete. But she dreaded what he might say.

"Did you really make that pie?" he asked, surprising her.

She turned from the sink to stare at him. "Yes, of course I did. Did you think Mom would lie about it?"

"Nope. I just didn't know you could cook."

Janie chuckled. "I'm not as good as Mom, but she made sure I wouldn't starve to death if I ever left home."

"Isn't that strange? If anyone had asked me, I would've said I knew everything there was to know about you. After all, I watched you grow up."

"There's lots you don't know about me," she assured him, amused by his words.

"Oh, yeah? Like what?"

"Do you know who gave me my first kiss?"

The sudden glower on his face tickled her, and she laughed.

"I don't find that question so funny," Pete said.

"I was just making a point."

He set a pile of dishes down beside her at the sink. "I need to ask you a question."

The sudden seriousness of his tone made her stomach clinch. "What?"

"Did you sleep with Manning?"

"I don't think that's any of your business."

"I know it's not, but—but he said the baby was his." Pete didn't look at her. He kept his gaze on the dishes in front of him.

"I thought you said you believed this is your baby. Have you changed your mind? If so, I bet you're glad I turned down your marriage proposal." She tried to keep her voice light, as if his answer didn't matter. Inside, her heart was breaking.

His hands, resting on the kitchen cabinet, clenched. "No, I don't think it's his baby. You wouldn't lie to me."

"Ah. Thanks for that, at least."

"What?"

"You think I'm a loose woman but an honest one."

"Janie! I didn't mean— You have every right to— I just wondered."

"Is that all of the dishes?" Maybe if they talked of mundane things, she could hold back the hunger that filled her.

"Uh, no. I'll get the rest of them."

She rinsed more dishes and was bent over, stacking them in the dishwasher, when Pete reached around her to catch her braid, hanging down in the open washer.

"Careful. You might get your hair caught on something."

The shivers that coursed up and down her body warned her again that Pete's touch had a tremendous effect on her. As if she could've forgotten. "Thanks. I'm—I'm thinking of cutting it."

"No!" Pete's voice was filled with horror.

She turned to stare at him. "It's just hair, Pete. It'll grow back."

A slow, sexy grin appeared on Pete's face. "Well, now, Janie, it may be just hair to you, but undoing your braid is one of my favorite memories. And when I'm holding you in my arms and those silken strands slide across my shoulders..." He paused and took a deep breath before finishing in a low voice, "I feel like I'm in heaven."

Janie fought the desire that filled her, that pleaded with her to turn into his arms, to feel his strength around her. She swallowed and licked her lips, playing for time.

"Aw, Janie, look at me."

She was powerless to refuse. Slowly she lifted her gaze to his, knowing that when she did so, he would kiss her. But she'd already expended her energy resisting him all evening.

When he pulled her against him, his big, hard body heating her skin even through their clothes, she gave in to her cravings and met him more than halfway. Still, the flash fire of desire that filled her was a surprise. Not that she hadn't always been sensitive to Pete's touch, but somehow she'd envisioned less interest in sex now that she was pregnant.

If anything, however, she was discovering her nerve endings were more finely tuned to the stimulus of his touch. When his lips left hers to trace the slender line of her neck, she gasped. Breathing became more and more difficult. Her hands roamed his broad shoulders as she clung to him.

"Janie, I need you," Pete muttered just before his lips returned to hers.

Her mind was racing as fast as her heart as she tried to respond to his words. She needed him, too, so much. But she needed more than his body. His heart was her goal, and she could settle for no less.

With a groan, she wrenched her lips from his. "Pete, we can't.... Mom and Dad—"

"If we're getting married, they wouldn't say anything," he said eagerly, his hands roaming her body with intensity.

"We're not getting married," she reminded him. She had to keep saying those words over and over again for her own sake as well as Pete's. It was too tempting to give in to his touch if she didn't.

"Damn it, Janie! How can you turn me down? We're good together. We're having a child. Marriage is the answer to everything."

"No, Pete. Love is the answer to everything. And you don't love me." She grabbed hold of the kitchen cabinet with both hands as she leaned against it, hoping to keep from reaching out to touch his tempting body.

"You know I don't believe in love."

"Why, Pete? Why don't you believe in love? Just because of Chloe? You're going to let one rotten apple spoil everything? Are you saying I'm like Chloe?" She stared at him, a challenge in her gaze.

"Of course you're not like Chloe! I never said that!"

"But you're lumping me in the same group as Chloe."

"Look, Janie, love doesn't last. People—people leave. It's better not to—"

"Who left you, Pete? Did you have a lover who left you?" She'd tried to follow his love life while he was on the ranch, but he'd gone away to college. And then he'd ridden the rodeo circuit.

He shrugged his shoulders. "I wasn't a virgin when we made love, Janie. But I'm certainly not going to give you a summary of my past love life."

Before her very eyes, she watched him withdraw, pull in, the eager lover disappearing. In his place was a withdrawn, hard man, protective of his secrets.

"Then how will I understand why you refuse to love me? Is it because I'm not lovable?"

"No!" he barked, anger in his eyes. "Janie, drop it! I want to take care of you and our baby. That's all you need to know."

"No, it's not. How old were you when your mother died?" She wasn't sure why that question popped into her head, but his reaction told her she'd touched a tender spot.

"My mother's death has nothing to do with us. Don't start talking like a shrink, Janie." Before she could say anything else, he turned toward the door. "I have to go. Tell your mom I said thanks for dinner."

Stunned by his abrupt about-face, Janie stood silent until he'd reached the back door. Then she remembered something she'd intended to tell him all along. "Pete?"

"Yeah?" he asked, but he kept his back to her.

"I didn't sleep with Bryan."

He remained still, as if frozen in place, for a few seconds. Then he walked out. She stood there, unable to move or react. Then as the door closed, Janie thought she heard a loud cowboy yell split the night air.

ALL THE WAY HOME, Pete tried to concentrate on his happiness. Janie hadn't slept with Bryan. Since she was a virgin when they'd begun their affair, he knew he had been her only lover. And he intended to keep it that way!

As much as he celebrated the good news, even more did he try to avoid thinking about Janie's questions. He knew the problem wasn't Janie—she was more lovable than anyone he'd ever met. The problem was with him. But he didn't think it was unusual for a man to resist loving a woman.

And he didn't want to think about it.

Unfortunately Jake was waiting for him when he got home. Waiting to talk about the upcoming marriage.

"Well? You haven't been at the grocery store all this time, have you?" Jake demanded when Pete walked into the kitchen.

"If he has, he's bought out the store," Brett teased his brother.

"No. I had dinner with the Dawsons. Sorry I didn't call, Red."

"That's all right. You can eat the leftovers for lunch tomorrow," Red assured him. He was busy at the kitchen counter while Pete's brothers sat at the table, their customary cups of coffee in front of them.

"So I guess Janie talked to you at the store." Jake said. "Did she agree to marry you?"

"No. And—and we didn't do much talking. Manning showed up right after I got there."

"So what did you do?" Brett asked.

"We helped her do her shopping."

"You and Manning?" Brett asked, as if he wasn't sure he'd heard his brother correctly.

Pete grinned. "Yeah. It wasn't pretty."

"What happened?" Red asked, coming to the table.

Pete ran a hand through his dark hair, wondering how to explain the escapade at the store. Finally, he just stated the facts.

"Mercy," Red muttered. "It's a wonder the girl's still speaking to you, much less inviting you to eat."

"Lavinia invited me. But Janie and I made up."

As always, Jake got back to the heart of the matter. "Then why won't she agree to marry you?"

Pete was saved from answering by the sound of a vehicle coming down the driveway. Everyone looked up in surprise. It was a cold, dark night in Wyoming, not a good night for visits.

Red went to the window, but whoever was arriving had already turned off his or her lights. Jake stood to go to the front of the house, assuming whoever had come would knock on the front door. Before he could leave the kitchen, however, the back door opened. There were two people there, but only one walked in . . . carrying the woman with him.

"Chad! Megan!" Brett exclaimed, and all the Randalls, plus Red, conducted a group hug. When they eventually separated, Chad, the youngest of the four Randall brothers, let his bride slide to the floor.

"Did we surprise you?" he asked.

"Yeah. Why didn't you call us to pick you up instead of renting a car?" Jake asked as he gestured to the table.

Chad and Megan sat down as Red poured two more cups of coffee. "We didn't fly. We drove," Chad explained.

"I wanted to bring a lot of things with me," Megan added.

"Of course, I hadn't thought of that," Jake agreed. "You'd need to move out of your apartment. Are you shipping the rest of it?"

Megan glanced at Chad before answering Jake. "I'm not giving up my apartment just yet, Jake."

"Why not? You two are living here, aren't you?"

There was a tense silence before Chad replied, "Jake, of course we're living here, but Megan wants to keep her job while her company does the work here, and she'll need to go back to Denver occasionally."

Pete watched the others, an amused smile on his lips. It was a relief to have someone else the center of Jake's attention. Ever since Jake had invited three decorators to redo the house, he'd been scheming to marry off his brothers.

When Chad and Megan, one of the decorators, fell in love and called to say they were marrying, Jake had been full of himself. Pete was as pleased as the rest of them for Chad's happiness, but he thought it might not be a bad idea for Jake to discover he wasn't in control of everything Randall.

"Keep her job?" Jake bellowed. He turned to his new sister-in-law. "Megan, you don't have to work. You and Chad will be wanting to start a family, like Pete here, and—"

Jake's words set off an uproar from Chad and Megan. Megan immediately protested Jake's dismissal of her job, and Chad wanted to know what Jake was talking about.

Questions flew around the table, but answers were in short supply until a sudden clanging got everyone's attention. Red was standing by the sink beating a skillet with a large spoon.

"Here, now! You all are gonna have to settle down or I'm kickin' you out of my kitchen."

Brett grinned at his oldest brother. "Guess Red's got a point. Maybe you'd better stop laying down the law and listen to what the newest member of the Randall clan wants."

Jake glared at his sibling, but he carefully wiped the frown away when he turned to Megan. She'd rapidly become a favorite with all of them even before they realized she'd be joining their family. "Megan, I didn't mean to step on any toes. I just assumed—"

"Sorry, Jake, but Chad and I haven't discussed—" her cheeks heated as she sought the right word "—starting a family. And I don't want to miss out on redoing the house. I'm looking forward to working with Adele." Adele, the second of the three decorators, was older, but she and Megan got along well. They'd decided to combine their ideas for the ranch house.

The other three brothers looked at Chad, as if wondering how he would react to his wife's response. Chad leaned back in his chair and grinned. "Boys, whatever makes Meggie happy is fine with me. Now, what's this about Pete?"

Pete immediately realized his time out of the spotlight had come to an end. But he left it to Jake to do the explaining.

"Janie's pregnant."

Talking about Janie and the baby made Pete tongue-tied, but even he could've done better than Jake's blunt statement.

Megan looked puzzled, but Chad put things together quickly and turned to Pete, a frown on his face. "Yours?"

Pete nodded.

"So, when's the wedding?"

With a sigh, Pete confessed, "I don't know."

"You offered, didn't you?" Chad demanded, tensing. "You can't treat Janie like some—some . . ."

"Of course I offered. Hell, I insisted. But you know Janie. She's as hardheaded as they come."

"You mean she turned you down?" Chad asked, astonishment on his face.

Pete studied his cup of coffee, and no one said anything.

Finally Megan reached out to pat Pete on the arm. "I'm looking forward to meeting Janie. I saw her the night you all took us to the steak house, but we weren't introduced."

"Maybe Megan could talk to her, woman to woman, you know?" Brett suggested.

Five pairs of male eyes focused on the only female in the room.

"Well," Megan said, before pausing to run her tongue over her lips, "I'd certainly like to—to talk to her, but I don't know—"

"Great!" Pete replied before she could finish. He was desperate for help. "I'll bring her over tomorrow."

Chapter Six

Chad settled beneath the covers with a sigh of satisfaction. Megan, emerging from the bathroom, noticed how much more comfortable her husband was here than in her apartment in Denver. "Happy to be home?"

He grinned, putting his big hands behind his head. "Yeah."

His muscular physique still took her breath away, but she tried to concentrate on other things. "You don't mind that I want to work on the house, do you?"

"Of course not. Like I said, whatever makes you happy."

"We haven't discussed children." She slipped off her robe and slid into the bed beside her handsome husband.

He chuckled and drew her into his arms. "Don't let Jake get to you, Meggie. I didn't marry you so we'd have another generation of Randalls. That's Jake's plan, not mine. I married you because I love you more than anything, even the ranch. Remember?"

She remembered. Afraid of marriage because of her mother's numerous trips down the aisle, she'd had a hard time believing Chad was serious about his commitment until he'd presented her with a prenuptial agreement promising her his share of the Randall ranch if he should ever leave her.

Offering her lips to assure him she remembered, Megan found herself wrapped in his powerful arms, his lips devouring hers.

When his mouth moved on to nibble on her neck, she asked, "But do you want children?"

He pulled back and stared at her in the night lamp's glow. "He really spooked you, didn't he?"

"No. But everything happened so quickly, I just realized we didn't discuss a lot of important things." She ran her fingers through the black hair on his chest, her gaze not meeting his until his fingers lifted her chin.

"You're not having regrets, are you?"

"No! Never!" Again she kissed him, with his complete cooperation. "But what do you think about children?"

Brushing back her silky hair, he said, "I think kids would be great, when you're ready. But Pete's taking care of the next generation, so there's no hurry."

"But what if she doesn't marry him?"

"She will. She's been in love with him forever." Then, with a laugh, he added, "Besides, Pete's got you on his side. You'll talk her into it."

Megan's eyes widened in panic just before Chad turned off the light and proceeded to distract her.

JANIE RODE OUT with her father the next morning, in spite of her mother's protests. "Mom, I'll be okay. I asked the doc, and he assured me any normal activities could be continued for a few more months. And Daddy needs me."

"I'll have a word with your father," Lavinia insisted.

"No, Mom. I'll be careful."

Lavinia knew her hardheaded daughter and gave up the fight, only saying a silent prayer that Janie was right. But she was relieved to find a like thinker when the phone rang about ten o'clock.

"Lavinia, may I speak to Janie?" Pete asked.

"She rode out with her father."

"What?" Pete roared. "What did you say?"

"Janie rode out with her father. She said he needed her help."

"Damnation! Crazy woman," Pete muttered.

Lavinia felt her regard for Pete rise until he asked his next question.

"Why didn't you stop her?"

"Pete Randall, you know Janie as well as I do. Do you think *you* could've stopped her if she'd made up her mind?"

"But the baby..."

"I *know*. She said the doc okayed it."

Pete muttered something else under his breath, but Lavinia didn't catch the words. And she decided not to ask him to repeat himself.

"Look, I called to see if all of you could come to dinner tonight," Pete finally said. "Chad and Megan are back home. I want Janie to meet her."

"I'm sure she'll want to meet Megan. But you don't have to include me and Hank."

"Janie wouldn't come without you." As if suddenly realizing how inhospitable his words sounded, Pete hastily added, "And we want you and Hank to meet Megan, too. After all, we're all going to be family."

"I hope so, Pete," Lavinia replied. "Shall we come about six?"

"That'll be great. See you then."

When Janie and her father returned for lunch, Lavinia repeated Pete's invitation.

"I don't think I'll go, thanks anyway," Janie said, sinking into a chair with a sigh of relief.

"Why not?" Hank demanded.

"Because I don't want to." She raised her chin and stared at her father.

"They're our neighbors, Janie Dawson. We'll all go. It's the neighborly thing to do." He joined her at the table as if the conversation were over.

"But, Daddy—"

"Janie, I think it's the least you can do. We've left the choice of marrying Pete up to you, but we shouldn't have to give up our association with the Randalls."

"Of course not, Mom, but I can stay at home, and you two—"

"We'll go as a family," Lavinia said firmly and sat down to dish up the food she'd prepared.

After a silent lunch, Janie decided not to return to the saddle with her father. Her mother let her help with the dishes and then shooed her upstairs. "You need a nap, young lady, and don't bother denying it."

With a weary smile, Janie shook her head. "I'm not a child, Mom...but you're right."

"I've been pregnant before. The most important thing now is your health."

"Yes, Mom."

As she started up the stairs, her mother added one more thing. "By the way, Pete was very unhappy that you were in the saddle this morning."

Janie was tempted to tell her mother what Pete could do with his concern, but she decided to save her words for the person who needed to hear them. Words she would deliver after a good nap.

HER AFTERNOON REST DID a lot to restore Janie's sense of humor. She could face Pete now and handle any arguments he threw at her concerning going about business as usual.

What she wasn't looking forward to was meeting the newest Randall. The bleached blonde who'd partied with the best of them that night at the steak house when she'd seen the Randall group from a distance hadn't impressed her.

The other decorator, an attractive young woman dressed in a classic fashion, had been clinging to Pete's hand. At least *she* wouldn't be there. Janie didn't want any competition for Pete's attention, much less competition that made her feel unattractive.

"Are you ready?" her father called up the stairs. "We don't want to be late."

He could speak for himself.

Janie joined her parents downstairs and apologized for keeping them waiting. On the drive over to the Randalls', she firmly kept the conversation on the running of the ranch. Her father loved to talk about business. According to him, the Dawson operation was the best in the state. He would allow the Randall spread, almost twice the size of theirs, to be second-best, but no better.

Light streamed out from the windows of the Randall homestead, welcoming them. The house was enormous, but it had become run-down over the years, under the care of only men. Janie hoped Chad's new wife did a better job with the house than she did with her own appearance.

The thought of Jake Randall facing chrome and glass at breakfast each morning, or relaxing in front of the fireplace in a lime green plastic beanbag chair, brought a chuckle to her lips. It might serve him right for his stupid matchmaking. Everyone in the county had heard the tale of his machinations.

And he'd intended for Pete to be the first married.

She drew a deep breath at such a scary thought.

"Everything okay?" Lavinia asked as Janie hesitated before getting out of the truck.

"Sure. I was just wondering how much Chad's wife would change the house."

Lavinia turned and stared at the stately home. "I hope not too much. It's always been beautiful."

"Come on, ladies. It's cold out here," Hank urged, placing a hand on each of their backs.

They allowed him to steer them toward the back door.

"Maybe we should go to the front door," Janie suggested. "After all, we're dinner guests."

Hank snorted but didn't change direction.

"I think we're okay at the back door. We've known them a long time," Lavinia said with a grin.

Since Pete emerged just then, they all knew they'd chosen the right door. He bounded off the porch and met them halfway.

"Hi. We're glad you could make it." He hugged Lavinia and shook Hank's hand. When he turned to Janie, she took a step back, but her hesitation didn't stop him. He hugged her close and brushed his lips across hers.

"Pete!" she protested.

"I was just saying hello. Come meet Megan. I think you'll like her."

Janie said nothing, but she wondered how men could be so blind. The bleached blonde she remembered, with her tight, suggestive clothing, might impress a room full of men, but Janie didn't think she'd appeal to either her or her mother.

When they entered the kitchen, only Red was there, busy at the stove. He turned to greet them, then quickly urged them into the living room.

"We're not eating in the kitchen?" Hank asked.

"Nope, we're formal tonight in Megan's honor," Red assured them. "We invited the vet and her aunt and little boy, too. That's too many to get around the table in here."

"The vet? I like B.J. I'll be glad of the chance to talk with her," Hank said.

"Her?" Lavinia asked, startled.

"Didn't I tell you she's a woman? Nice lady, very knowledgeable."

Janie looked at Pete. "Isn't she living on the ranch?"

"Yeah" was his brief answer.

"So the Randall ranch, after having no women for a quarter of a century, suddenly has two?"

Red was the one who answered her question. "More'n that if you count Mildred—I mean, Miss Bates—and I think you should."

Pete nodded but had nothing to say as he led them toward the living room.

When they entered the large room, the family was gathered around the fireplace. Everyone stood and turned to greet them, and Janie received a shock.

The bleached blonde wasn't there. But the beautiful woman who'd clung to Pete's hand was.

Chad came forward to greet them, pulling the fashionable young woman with him. Janie tried to suppress the surge of envy over the woman's elegant hairstyle, her knit skirt and sweater in a heavenly blue, the look of adoration Chad was giving her.

"I'd like to present my wife, Megan," Chad was saying, and Janie managed a nod in greeting.

Lavinia and Hank shook her hand, and then it was Janie's turn. "Hello, Megan. Welcome to Wyoming."

"Thank you, Janie. I know we haven't met, but I saw you that night at the steak house. I'm delighted to finally meet you."

"Me, too. But I'll confess to being confused. You were holding Pete's hand that night. I thought Chad had married the other lady."

"Rita?" Chad asked before hooting in derision. "I'm insulted, Janie, that you would think I'd pick someone like her. My heart was set on Megan from the first."

Janie managed a smile. "Well, I think you've chosen well."

Megan must have realized her discomfort, because she leaned closer and whispered, "I was only holding Pete's hand because he seemed so distressed to see you with another man."

Janie smiled her thanks as Pete returned to her side to lead them to chairs by the fireplace. Red entered at that moment with some chips and salsa.

"Red, is there anything I can do to help?" Lavinia asked.

"Well, now, I could use a little help with the rolls, Lavinia, if you're sure."

"When I offered, he refused," an older woman said, sniffing in disdain at the man.

"Now, Miss Bates, this is your first time to dine with us, and I wanted—"

"Red, why don't Miss Bates and I both help you? I'd like to get to know one of our new neighbors." Lavinia sent an inviting smile to the lady, who immediately stood and joined Lavinia. The two walked out of the room, talking together, and Red followed behind, mumbling under his breath.

"Janie, that was Mildred, B.J.'s aunt, and here's B.J. and Toby," Pete said, gesturing to a tall woman a little older than Megan.

Janie shook hands and felt a lot more comfortable with B.J. than she did with Megan. B.J. was dressed in a denim skirt and blouse. She was one of their kind.

The little boy, adorable with his shyness, reminded Janie of the child she was carrying. Suddenly misty-eyed, she decided to sit down.

"You okay?" Pete whispered, hovering. "You shouldn't have ridden out with your dad today."

Janie glared at him. "You've always urged me on, telling me I didn't get any special privileges because I was a girl."

"That's when you were growing up. Not now. You're pregnant, damn it!" He'd stopped whispering somewhere in the middle of his protest, and his words rang out in the utter silence as he finished.

Janie tried to keep hold of her temper. "Thank you, Pete. I guess now I don't have to send out announcements." Then she smiled at the rest of those in the room, determined to avoid heavy drama. "You're in the company of a sinful woman, so let me know if I need to leave."

B.J. became her friend for life as she chuckled and said, "Honey, if you're the only woman the Randall clan has tempted to sin, I'll be surprised."

Megan joined her. "I'm certainly not going to cast any stones. Something about glass houses."

Jake had the final word. "We want to celebrate the newest Randall-to-be, Janie, not condemn him or her."

"Thank you." She could've pointed out that her baby was a Dawson, but that would be like a Southerner firing the first shot of the Civil War smack in the middle of Central Park.

Pete pulled a chair up to the side of hers and sat down, but he didn't have anything to say. He'd already said too much.

THE DINNER WAS more enjoyable than Janie had thought it would be. She discovered that Megan, in spite of her elegant city appearance, was warmhearted. Even better, the love she felt for Chad was written all over her.

So when Megan announced that Red shouldn't have to clean up since he'd done all the cooking, Janie was able to join the dishwashing crew with no qualms.

Or so she thought.

When the rest of the company had returned to the living room, Janie found herself left alone with Megan and B.J. For a few minutes, the three of them divided up the labor and chatted about the evening and the neighborhood.

Then, just as Janie began washing the dishes and B.J. dried while Megan put away the leftovers, the subject matter changed.

"Janie, this is a personal question, but I can tell you care for Pete." Megan hesitated by her side, a worried look on her face. "So why won't you marry him?"

B.J., after a sharp look at Megan, added, "And I know he cares for you."

Janie didn't want to answer. She didn't want to defend her position again. Nor did she want to expose her pain to anyone. Finally, however, she couldn't ignore the caring in their eyes and their words. "Does he?"

"I'd swear he does, especially since he learned about the baby," B.J. said. "I haven't known him long, but he seems to really want to take care of the two of you."

"Yes." Janie sighed and then turned to face the other two and said abruptly, "I asked him to marry me."

Megan gasped, but B.J. didn't show any reaction, so Janie assumed she already knew the story.

"You did? Then what's the problem?" Megan demanded.

"He turned me down."

After staring at her as if she could read the secret on Janie's face, Megan confessed, "I'm confused."

"He turned me down until I told him about the baby. He's willing to marry me for the baby's sake. Not because of me."

"I WONDER WHAT they're talking about," Pete whispered to Chad.

Everyone was gathered around the fireplace again, drinking coffee, while the three young women did the cleaning. Pete would've preferred being in the kitchen, even if it meant he had to wash the dishes. He didn't want Janie out of his sight.

"Don't worry. I told Megan to work on her. She'll probably talk her into marrying you before the table's cleared off."

"What makes you so confident Megan can succeed where I can't?" Pete demanded a little huffily. *He* should be the one to persuade Janie, not Megan.

"She convinced a stubborn bachelor to marry, didn't she?" Chad boasted, looking irritatingly content.

"Yeah, but those techniques won't work on Janie," Pete muttered.

"What are you two whispering about?" Hank demanded.

"Hank, that's none of your business," Lavinia warned.

"Hank's right," Jake intervened. "They shouldn't be whispering in company."

"It's no big secret," Chad said, ignoring Pete's whispered protest. "I asked Megan to help convince Janie she should marry this old buzzard." He slapped Pete on the back and chuckled.

"Good," Hank replied. "I'd like a wedding real soon."

"I won't have Janie pressured," Lavinia insisted.

"Pressured, hell!" Hank roared. "It's her duty. She owes my grandchild, if nothing else."

"The most important thing is Janie and the baby's health," Lavinia said.

Pete's heart contracted in fear. "Is anything wrong? The doctor didn't see a problem, did he?"

"No, Pete. But I had some difficulties, as you know. I want to be sure Janie's healthy."

Somehow, in spite of knowing Lavinia's history, Pete hadn't connected it to Janie. Now anxiety was added to his frustration. "When does she go back to the doc?"

"I believe he's scheduled her for a sonogram next week."

"A sonogram? That early? Are you sure he doesn't suspect something is wrong?"

Mildred spoke up. "I believe they're using those right away now. Even when B.J. was pregnant with Toby, she had one early."

"What's a sonogram?" Toby asked, stumbling over the unfamiliar word.

Jake, who was sitting next to Mildred and Toby, reached over to rub the child's head. "It's a picture of you while you were in your mommy's tummy."

"Oh. Can I see it?"

Jake looked at Mildred, his eyebrow raised in question.

"We'll have to ask your mommy," Mildred replied.

"I want to go with Janie to Doc Jacoby's," Pete said. He didn't want secondhand information about his own child.

"If you do that, everyone will know the baby is yours," Lavinia warned.

"Damn it!" Pete yelled, standing. "Why does everyone think I don't want my identity known? This kid is mine! Janie is mine! And I'll fight the first person who dares say otherwise!"

Brett chuckled. "Janie was right. With Pete around, she won't need to send out birth announcements." He was unperturbed when Pete glared at him. "Don't waste your energy on me, big brother. I'm all for Janie marrying you."

"We all are," Lavinia assured him, "if it's Janie's choice. But if she doesn't marry you, Pete, I promise you we'll take good care of her and the baby."

Pete sank back into his chair, misery filling him. "I appreciate that, Lavinia, and I'm sorry I lost my temper. But *I* want to take care of my own. My family." Those two words filled him, making his heart swell with feelings he didn't want to admit to. He was only doing his duty, he promised himself.

"Don't worry. Megan will persuade Janie, I'm sure," Chad assured him with a grin.

At that moment, the door opened and the three young women entered the room.

"We've finished the dishes. Does anyone need a fresh cup of coffee?" Megan asked, smiling at everyone.

"No," Hank replied, rising. "What we need is a yes from Janie. Did you talk her into it?" His frankness rendered his audience silent.

Pete watched, holding his breath, his gaze glued to Janie, but she didn't look at him.

Megan, after drawing a deep breath, replied, "No. I didn't. In fact, I agree with Janie. She shouldn't marry Pete."

Chapter Seven

Pete paced the floor the length of the telephone cord while he waited for someone to answer the Dawsons' phone. When Hank finally growled into the receiver, Pete breathed a sigh of relief. If Janie or her mother had answered, either of them might have hung up the phone rather than talk to him after the brouhaha two nights ago.

"Hank, I need to know when Janie's going to the doctor."

"I don't think I'm supposed to tell you."

"Come on, Hank. I need to go with her."

"Look, boy, I'm already sleeping on the sofa because of you. I don't think—" He stopped, and Pete waited for him to continue. "Aw, hell, okay. She has an appointment at three this afternoon. She and her mother left the house about five minutes ago."

"Damn! Okay, okay, I'll drive into town and meet them there." As an afterthought, he added, "If it makes you feel any better, you're not the only one suffering from the other night. Chad is having problems, too."

"Good. That boy needs to learn a few things about women."

Pete thought that was pretty much a case of the pot calling the kettle black, but he didn't say so. "I guess we all need help understanding females, Hank."

Hank grunted his agreement before saying, "You'd better get moving if you're going to be there in time."

"Yeah. Thanks, Hank."

"You bet. We men gotta stick together. Besides, I'm already on the couch. How much worse can it get?"

Pete didn't attempt to answer that question. He only hoped Hank didn't find out.

Grabbing his coat as he told Red he was going into town, Pete rushed out the back door to his truck. He was grateful he'd called Hank when he had. He'd been tempted to wait a few more days, so that everyone's temper might have cooled a bit more. The dinner two nights ago had ended in a male-versus-female battle.

He wasn't sure Janie would even speak to him. How she would react when he showed up at Doc Jacoby's office he didn't know.

Squaring his jaw, Pete vowed nothing would stop him from taking care of his baby and his... Janie.

When he entered Doc Jacoby's waiting room and all eyes of the waiting patients focused on him, he had to remember his resolve. After pausing, he strode over to the window to announce his arrival.

"Well, hi Pete. What are you doing here? You got a touch of the flu that's going around?" asked Mandy

Andrews, the doctor's receptionist who'd gone to school with all the Randall brothers and Janie.

"Uh, no."

She waited, looking at him expectantly, for more information.

"I need to see the doc."

Grinning, she said, "Well, I figured that. Otherwise, you wouldn't be here."

She continued to stare at him, and Pete realized he was going to have to explain his presence. Feeling his cheeks heat up, he sought for the least embarrassing way.

Mandy's eyebrows suddenly shot up, and she leaned forward. "Don't tell me you've got one of those diseases?"

"No!" The eagerness in her voice told him she was ready to broadcast the news to the entire town. So what? He'd said he wanted to claim his baby. Squaring his shoulders, he said, "Is Janie here? I want to be with Janie during the examination."

"Now, Pete, I know the Randalls and Dawsons have been friends a long time, but her mother is with her. Why, the only way I'd let you in is if you were the—"

"I am."

Mandy's eyes widened, but she said nothing except to excuse herself.

Only seconds later, as Pete stood at the window, not knowing what to do with himself, Mrs. Priddy, Doc's starchy nurse, appeared.

"Young man, are you claiming to be the father of Janie Dawson's baby?" she asked in a whisper that could've reached the back rows of any theater. There was a sudden hush around him.

Again he straightened and said, "Yes, I am, and I want to be with her during the examination."

"She didn't say you would be coming."

"I'm here." He certainly wasn't going to start explaining all the complications of his and Janie's relationship.

After glaring at him, Mrs. Priddy muttered, "Wait here."

Like I have a choice, Pete groused to himself. The door into the examining rooms was kept locked. He remained by the window, ignoring Mandy's surreptitious stares as she resumed her place in front of the computer.

Finally, when he thought he could stand the waiting no longer, the magic door opened.

"Mr. Randall," Mrs. Priddy called out, and he hurried to the door.

"This way, please."

Without saying another word, she led him down the hallway to a closed door. The smells of medicine and antiseptic surrounded him, reminding him of visits to the doc as a child. Mrs. Priddy seemed just as forbidding today as she had back then.

And he wouldn't get a lollipop today.

She swung open a door, and he stiffened his shoulders, prepared to face Janie's wrath.

Instead, he found himself in the doctor's office. Doc Jacoby was sitting behind a massive desk, a frown on his face.

"Come on in, Pete, and have a seat."

"I want to see Janie," Pete blurted out, not moving from the doorway.

"Yes, so Priddy told me. She also said you're the father of Janie's baby."

"Yes."

"Janie didn't mention to Priddy that you'd be coming." Bright blue eyes stared at him from beneath bushy white eyebrows.

To give himself time to think, Pete moved to the chair in front of Doc's desk and sat down. "I, uh, we've had some differences of opinion. She refuses to marry me, seems to think I'm ashamed of the baby," Pete announced, his voice rising with frustration.

"And you're not?"

"Hell, no! I've begged her to marry me. I told her I'd shout the fact that this is my baby from the rooftops. She keeps saying no."

"Hmm," Doc Jacoby muttered, one finger laid across his lips. Then he stood up and Pete did, too. "Sit down, boy. I'll go talk to Janie and her mother. You wait here."

"I'm tired of waiting. I'll go with you."

"You'll wait here as I said, or I'm turning Priddy loose on you with a syringe."

Pete collapsed in the chair.

"WHEN IS HE GOING TO COME?" Janie finally demanded. She'd been patient as long as she could be.

"Doc will be in as soon as he can, Janie. You know that. Just relax." Lavinia sat in a chair nearby the examining table, a magazine spread across her lap.

But Janie wasn't fooled. Lavinia had been turning the pages at random. Janie didn't think her mother had seen a single page.

"Mom, I wish you wouldn't be mad at Dad," Janie burst out. "Ever since dinner at the Randalls', life at home has been crazy."

"Don't concern yourself. Punishment won't hurt your father." Lavinia grinned. "And it's not the first time."

"But I feel so bad about everyone getting upset. B.J. called yesterday. She said Chad and Megan are hardly speaking."

"At least B.J.'s not having marital problems."

"Only because she doesn't have a husband. But what if Jake decides to take her house away?"

"Jake Randall may be upset, but he won't be unfair. You know better than that. The Randalls are good men, even if they don't understand women."

"Do you think it has anything to do with their mother's death?" Janie asked, returning to the question she'd asked Pete after their grocery shopping.

"Possibly. Jake and Pete were at very impressionable ages. Pete was five and Jake eight. Old enough to realize that their mother had left them, even if they couldn't understand death." Lavinia frowned and then began, "Maybe—"

Doc Jacoby's entry stopped her.

"Hi there, young lady, Lavinia."

Lavinia greeted her old friend, but Janie only smiled nervously.

"Janie, my girl, we have a small problem," the doctor began.

Janie covered her stomach with her hand. "My baby?"

"No, child, no. We haven't done the sonogram yet, remember? No, the problem is with the daddy."

Janie stiffened and looked away.

"What do you mean?" Lavinia asked.

"Well, Pete Randall is waiting in my office. He claims to be the father of this child and wants to be present during the sonogram."

"No!" Janie replied sharply.

"No what? No, he isn't the father, or no, you don't want him to be present?"

Janie didn't look at the doctor. She didn't want to face the kind man who'd taken care of all her physical ailments since her birth. With her head down, she finally muttered, "He's the father, but I don't want him here."

Before Lavinia could say anything—and Janie could sense her intent as she stirred—Doc Jacoby responded. "Now, Janie, I believe a woman should have control over her own body. If you tell me to send Pete away, I will. But I think you ought to reconsider your decision. This is his child, too. Even if you don't want to have anything to do with him, I think he should know about his baby."

Janie thought he should, too. But she didn't want to lie down on a table, her clothing removed, and allow Pete to stare at her stomach. Yet she guessed she didn't have any choice. Swallowing the sudden lump in her throat, she whispered, "Okay."

Lavinia reached out and squeezed her hand in support, and Janie dared lift her gaze to her mother and offer a weak smile.

"Good girl," Doc said, patting her on the shoulder. "You put on the gown Priddy left for you and lie down on the table. I'll knock before I bring Pete in."

As soon as the doctor left the room, Mrs. Priddy replaced him, leaving mother and daughter no time to talk alone. But Janie knew she'd pleased her mother with her choice.

The gown, pink crinkle paper, was different from those she'd worn in the past. This one had snaps down the front, which would allow the doctor access to her stomach without revealing much else, thankfully. When a knock came on the door, she squeezed her eyes closed.

"Just relax, Janie. The doctor will take care of you," Mrs. Priddy assured her.

It wasn't the doctor making her tense.

"All right, Janie, I think everyone is here. We'll begin the show," Doc Jacoby boomed. Janie didn't have to see him to know he was smiling.

"Actually," Lavinia said, "it feels a bit crowded in here. Why don't I wait in the reception room?"

Janie's eyes popped open, and she pleaded without speaking for her mother not to abandon her. But Lavinia carefully averted her gaze.

"Lavinia, I'll be glad to bring Janie home, if you want. I'll be real careful," Pete promised.

"Thanks, Pete, if you're sure you don't mind. I can go on home and start making dinner. You'll join us, won't you?"

"Mom!" Janie finally protested, but the other two ignored her.

"Thanks, Lavinia. I'd appreciate that."

Before Janie could think of anything to say, Lavinia slipped from the room.

"You don't mind, do you, Janie?" Pete finally asked.

"You mean now that it's too late, I get to voice my opinion?" she demanded.

"Calm down, Janie," Doc urged. "Your blood pressure is going to shoot through the roof."

"She has blood-pressure problems?" Pete asked anxiously.

"No, I don't have blood-pressure problems!" Janie retorted.

Doc Jacoby heaved a big sigh. "Pete, you go sit down in that chair," he said, pointing to the chair Lavinia had occupied. "You," he began, turning back to Janie, "lie back and relax. I have other patients waiting."

Janie did as she was told, allowing her gaze to roam to Pete, waiting tensely in the chair, before closing her eyes again.

"Okay, Janie, I'm going to open your robe so I can examine you," Doc said even as he unsnapped the gown over her stomach. Then he began pressing on her stomach, making her regret the two glasses of iced tea she'd had at lunch.

When he grunted after placing the cold stethoscope to her stomach, she felt movement and opened her eyes to find Pete standing over her on the other side of the table.

"Is everything all right?"

Doc frowned at him. "Hmm? Oh, yes, yes, everything's fine. Quit worrying, boy."

Pete picked up her hand and threaded his fingers through hers. Janie tried to pretend that she didn't like the touch, but she knew she was lying to herself. Pete's grasp tightened as she clung to him.

"Okay, Priddy, let's prep her for the sonogram," the doctor muttered.

Mrs. Priddy, her lips pressed tightly together, came into Janie's range of vision and began smearing some kind of petroleum jelly on her stomach.

"What's that for?" Pete demanded, asking the question Janie was wondering.

"It helps conduct the transmission." The doctor patted the small black machine on a cart. "This contraption is something else. With the doctor in the next county sharing the expense, we've improved the care for all our expectant mothers." He beamed at Janie as if expecting a thank-you.

But she remained silent, waiting for the examination. Thoughts of her mother's difficulties, combined with the tension of the past week, had her dwelling on the negatives of her situation.

Doc Jacoby took a ball connected with wires to the machine and began rolling it around Janie's stomach. She even feared he might hurt the baby by pressing so hard.

"Doc—" Pete began, and then he stopped, but his hold on Janie's hand tightened. Since the doctor ignored him, he said again, "Doc, shouldn't you be more gentle?"

"You got experience with babies, son? Until you do, keep your advice to yourself." He watched the machine as he continued to move the ball. Then he exclaimed, "Aha!"

"What is it?" Pete demanded.

"See that? That's a heartbeat. That's your child, Pete Randall, alive and well."

"Doctor," Mrs. Priddy whispered, elbowing him and pointing to the machine.

"What? What?" Pete insisted, looking from the doctor to the nurse and back again. Janie followed his gaze, apprehension filling her.

"Well, well, well. I thought that might be true," Doc muttered to himself as he changed the position of the ball slightly.

"Doc, if you don't tell us right now what's wrong, I'm gonna—" Pete broke off, and Janie suspected he couldn't think of a threat Doc Jacoby would believe.

"Nothing's wrong. I told you that. But I do have some news. I don't know whether you'll think it's good news or bad, but—"

"Doc!" Pete roared.

"You're having twins."

PETE STARED AT THE MAN he'd known all his life as if he were a stranger. "What did you say?"

Doc Jacoby looked at both of them, a beaming smile on his face. "Twins. I said twins. I haven't delivered a set of twins in five or six years. The last ones were, um, what were their names? They moved right afterward. Remember, Priddy?"

"The Blackwells," Mrs. Priddy said crisply.

"Right, right. The Blackwells. Nice family. I remember—"

"Doc!" Pete roared again. "Forget the Blackwells. What about Janie . . . and the babies? Are they all right?"

"Well, a'course they are. Don't you see those strong heartbeats?" Doc pointed to the screen.

Pete stared at the dual thumping, finding it hard to believe that they represented his children. Children! He was having not one but two babies.

He lifted Janie's hand to his lips. "You okay, Janie?"

She, too, was staring in fascination at the machine. "Could there be some mistake, Doc? I mean, it's still early."

"No, Janie, no mistake. You've got two little buns in the oven. And I'm thinking you may be further along than I thought. Maybe closer to nine weeks than seven."

Pete watched Janie as she took in Doc's words. When her gaze flew to his face and then quickly away, he knew she was remembering their argument and the passionate making-up. The sudden longing that filled him to hold her again almost made him forget the news.

"I guess your mother is going to be surprised," he murmured, both his hands holding hers against his chest.

"Happily surprised, I hope?" Doc asked, his smile having gradually disintegrated. "You two are happy, aren't you?"

Janie stared at the doctor, seemingly speechless, and Pete squeezed her hand. "Of course we are, Doc. It's the shock, that's all."

As if realizing Janie needed some time alone, Mrs. Priddy urged the doctor to take Pete to his office while Janie dressed. The two professionals exchanged a look that Pete didn't quite understand.

"Janie will come to Doc's office when she's dressed?" he asked, wanting to be sure she didn't leave. "I'm taking her home."

"Yes, Pete, we know," Mrs. Priddy assured him, patting him on the arm. Then she pushed him and Doc out the door.

"That woman can herd people better than anyone I know," Doc muttered as he led Pete to his office.

Once they were seated, Pete leaned forward. "You didn't hide anything from us, did you, Doc? Janie's going to be all right?"

"As far as I can tell. A lot of things can happen in the next seven months. Maybe less. Twins usually come early." He smiled reassuringly at Pete. "What are you going to do about all this?"

"What do you mean?"

"I mean, are you going to marry Janie or not? Twins can be a heavy burden for a single parent."

"Damn it, Doc, I've been pleading with her to marry me. Both families are up in arms, the men arguing with the women, about our getting married. I don't know what else to do."

"Well, she must have some reason for turning you down. What is it?"

"It's personal," Pete snapped. He didn't intend to share his and Janie's private difficulties with the doctor.

Before Doc could question him further, making him feel he was back home facing Jake, the door opened and Janie slipped into the room.

"Sit right here, my dear," Doc said, gesturing to the chair beside Pete. "We need to go over a few things."

Pete couldn't stand the apprehensive look on her face. He reached out and took her hand again. To his surprise, she didn't protest.

"I'm giving you a prescription for vitamins that you are to take faithfully. Those two babies are going to need a lot of nourishment. Are you throwing up?"

"No."

"Janie, the other day you threw up," Pete reminded her.

The glare she sent him told him she didn't appreciate his help.

"That was because of—of tension, not morning sickness."

"Hmm," Doc said, watching her closely, "Okay, we won't worry about that so far. But if it starts happening, Janie, you let me know. Priddy says you've already lost four pounds since last week."

"She has?" Pete asked, straightening in his chair. "Should she be doing that? I thought women gained weight when they were pregnant."

"She'll gain weight, Pete. Some women lose early on, but we'll monitor Janie's progress. And you, young lady, I want you to get plenty of rest. Take a nap every afternoon and go to bed early. Once you get beyond the first three months, you won't be quite so tired, but don't push yourself.''

''Yes, Doc.''

Pete thought Janie sounded subdued, and he wanted to pull her into his arms, to comfort her. Then he thought of something else he needed to ask.

''What about horse riding, Doc? Shouldn't she give that up until after—after the babies are born?''

''I told you Doc said it was okay!'' Janie said, firing up at his interference.

''You're right, I did. But I think maybe it's not such a good idea now, Janie. Twins change things a little.''

A little? Pete thought they changed things a lot.

After a few more last-minute instructions, Pete led Janie to his pickup. He helped her in and then hurried around to the driver's side. ''Shall we go get the prescription filled before we go home, Janie? It will save you a trip tomorrow. And you probably should start the vitamins as soon as possible.''

''Fine.''

Pete headed to the drugstore, but he didn't give all his attention to his driving. ''Are you upset about the twins?'' he asked.

''No.''

''Then what's wrong? You're not saying much. Did Doc hurt you? I thought he wasn't as gentle as he could've been.''

''No, Pete, he didn't hurt me. It—it's just a shock, like you said.''

He parked in front of the drugstore. "Janie, I know you don't want to marry me, but that doesn't mean I'm going to abandon you or forget that these babies are mine, too. I'll do everything I can to help you." Leaning over, he brushed her lips with his, aching to deepen the kiss, to celebrate the incredible news that they were having twins. But he did neither.

Janie said nothing.

"Wait here. I'll be right back."

And he was. There was no one waiting, and the pharmacist filled the vitamin prescription at once, even though he sent several curious looks in Pete's direction.

Pete hurried back to the truck. "Guess we'd better be on our way and tell your parents before gossip beats us to it," he suggested with a wry chuckle.

"We have something else to tell them, too."

"What's that, sweetheart?" he asked as he backed out of the parking space.

"I've decided to marry you—if you still want me after you hear my terms."

Chapter Eight

Even as she finished speaking, Janie was holding her breath. But when Pete threw on the brakes, practically standing on them, she had to forget her breathing to grab hold of the armrest. Otherwise, she would've ended up on the floorboard.

"You'll marry me?" he demanded.

"Yes," Janie said, breathing deeply. "But only on one condition, Pete. And you won't like it."

She'd given her decision some thought since Doc had told her she was having twins. Suddenly overwhelmed, she'd realized she would need Pete's strength, as well as her own, to give her babies a healthy birth. And he deserved to be involved in his children's lives.

And then there was the fighting in their families.

And the fact that she didn't think she could hold out much longer between Pete's pursuit and her longings.

"What condition?"

Before she could answer, loud honking interrupted. They both turned to see several cars lined up behind them on the road.

Pete quickly pulled the truck into the same parking place. "What condition?" he repeated.

"I'll understand if you say no, Pete. Really, I will. But I can't—I can't sleep with you." After one look at the shock on his face, she turned away and waited for his response.

One large hand snaked out to pull her chin back around to him. "Let me get this straight. You'll marry me, but you won't sleep with me?"

Her skin tingled from his touch, and she could understand his incredulity. She'd always responded to him like fire racing through deadwood. "Yes."

"Janie, that's absurd! If there was one thing right about us, it was the loving."

"But it wasn't loving, Pete. Remember? You don't love me. You just want me."

"Don't start that again, Janie. I want to take care of you and our baby—babies. That's enough."

What a hardheaded man. She wanted his love so badly, she'd been willing to risk giving him up. But he hadn't budged an inch. "Pete, you can say no. I won't tell anyone. Everyone will continue to think I'm being stubborn."

"You are!" he snapped.

She didn't think he had to be so quick with his agreement. "Fine. We'll just forget I ever offered."

"Nope, we won't. I'm accepting your proposal," Pete said firmly. "I'm marrying you. But I have a condition, too."

Such a jumble of emotions filled Janie. She was going to marry Pete Randall. But he had terms. Just like her. "What—what kind of terms?"

"I don't want anyone to know that our marriage isn't a normal one. I'll go along with your terms until after the babies are born. I'm not sure it'd be safe, anyway. Then we'll renegotiate. Okay?"

"Renegotiate?" she repeated, her voice wavering.

His eyes narrowed, and he reached out to encircle her nape. "That's right, Janie, my girl. You get your way now. I get my way later."

"Wait—" In one fluid motion, he pulled her close, and his lips covered hers. Instantly the longing that welled up in her was more than she could handle. She'd never realized before that life without Pete's touch was colorless.

Her fingers fluttered against his cheeks before sliding around his neck. She settled into his embrace with a sigh that shivered all the way through her. How she'd missed his kisses! When his tongue pressed for entry, she didn't hesitate. The taste of him was ambrosia to her.

His hands stroked her sides under her coat, then slid around to cup her breasts. Memories of their lovemaking overtook her. Pete had never done anything halfway. When he'd taken her, she'd felt completely loved—and she longed to feel that way again.

Hazily she tried to remember why they'd stopped loving each other. It felt so good. *He* felt so good. She slid one hand down across his broad chest, her fingers seeking an opening so she could touch his warm skin.

But her tactile exploration was cut short when a rapping on the car window interrupted their embrace. Pete looked over her shoulder and grinned at the old gentleman passing by. But Janie couldn't even summon up a smile. Now she remembered why she hadn't felt Pete's arms around her for a long time—and why she'd agreed to marry him but not sleep with him.

Pete's loving might be magical, but reality hurt too much afterward. It was a lot safer to do without his touch, she reminded herself as she fought to stay in control of her emotions.

As if he were obliging her, he immediately set the truck in motion again, pulling out of the parking space with a squeal of tires.

"Slow down, Pete," Janie protested. "What's the hurry?"

"What's the hurry? I'm getting you home in front of your parents before you change your mind."

Janie drew a deep breath. The ramifications of her offer were beginning to sink in. "I—I won't change my mind, but we could wait awhile, to see if you do."

"I won't. And we're not waiting."

"Well, you don't have to be so dictatorial!"

Pete pressed down on the accelerator. "Dictatorial? Janie Dawson, I've been following you around like a dog begging for a bone for almost a week. And you wonder why I don't want to wait?"

"I'm not showing yet."

"No, but at least ten people heard Mrs. Priddy ask me if I was the daddy. So just how long do you think that secret will take to spread all over the county?"

"You said you didn't mind if people knew," she reminded him, her teeth sinking into her bottom lip.

"Hell, Janie! You're driving me crazy. I'm thinking about you, not me. People always blame the woman, you know that. If we get married at once, there won't be that much gossip. But if we wait, after everyone knows, they'll think you forced me to marry you." He grinned, a teasing look in his eyes that reminded her of happier times.

"Maybe I'll tell them *you* forced *me*."

"And that would be accurate," he returned, and then puffed out his chest. "But no one would believe you."

Only the laughter on his face kept her from slugging him. He had always teased her. "A little full of yourself, aren't you?"

"Why not? I'm having twins . . . and I'm marrying the most beautiful girl in the world."

Before she could recover from such a wonderful compliment, he leaned over and kissed her again.

"Pete! You're driving!"

"No problem. There aren't any cars."

"And—and we aren't going to do that." She was becoming concerned about the way he kept touching her, throwing her hormones into overdrive . . . and her control out the window.

"You're wrong about that, Janie. We have to convince everyone that we're a normal couple, remember? That was my condition, and you agreed. We may not have sex, but we'll be doing a lot of kissing."

Oh, mercy, she was in trouble.

"PERFECT TIMING," Lavinia called out as they entered. "Hank is washing up, and dinner is almost ready."

"Good. I'm starved," Pete said with a grin. He gave Janie a significant look, warning her to wait until her father arrived on the scene.

"Everything's okay?" Lavinia asked with a slight frown, as if sensing some underlying tension.

"Fine," Pete responded, not giving Janie a chance to speak. Hank came into the kitchen just then, and Pete was glad. He wasn't sure how long he and Janie could remain silent.

"You're back. How's everything, Janie?"

Janie looked at Pete and then her parents. "We—we have some news."

Hank, who had just started to sit down, straightened quickly. "You mean you're—"

"Having twins," Janie said breathlessly, her gaze going from her father to her mother.

As if Samantha in "Bewitched" had twitched her nose, everyone froze. Then, with a small cry, Lavinia hugged Janie, while Hank gasped like a marathon runner on his last mile.

After they expressed their concerns and happiness, Hank turned to the next topic. "Now, see here, Janie, I don't care what your reasons are, it's time you gave in and married Pete."

"She has," Pete said quietly—and, he'd admit, with a little pride. While everyone had tried to convince Janie, or at least all the men in the two families, he'd been the one to persuade her. He set aside his disappointment that she didn't really want him. He'd deal with that emotion later.

For the second time, they stunned Lavinia and Hank. Then the real celebration began. Lavinia had tears in her eyes as she served dinner, constantly asking questions about their decision.

Hank, relief on his face, served himself large portions of the steak and potatoes Lavinia had prepared, ignoring the broccoli.

"Hank Dawson, you put back that second steak. It has too much cholesterol. You want to be around to play with your grandbabies, don't you?" Lavinia asked sharply.

Hank rolled his eyes and replaced the smaller of the two steaks. "You watch out, Pete. Don't let Janie get the upper hand. You never get it back."

Lavinia ignored her husband's comment. "Have you told Pete's family yet?"

"No, Mom. I wanted you and Dad to be the first ones to know," Janie replied.

Actually they hadn't even discussed whom to tell first. Pete, too, had assumed they would tell her parents first. Now he was anxious to inform his own family.

"I think we should all go to the Randalls'. There's a lot to discuss. Is that all right with you, Pete?"

"That's a good idea, Lavinia. I'll call." Pete excused himself and went to the phone on the wall. Brett answered. "Brett, would you tell Red I'm eating at the Dawsons again?"

"Sure. But he may be mad."

"I know. But we're all coming over there after dinner. Tell Jake, will you?"

"Yeah. What's up?"

"I'll tell you when I get there."

He hung up as Brett asked him another question. They'd all find out together. And hopefully the news would bring peace back to the Randall household.

B.J. RAPPED on the back door and waited in the cold night for someone to open the door. She smiled when Megan urged her inside. The two women had talked several times since the disastrous dinner to welcome Megan and Chad. B.J. felt she'd made a new friend.

"How's it going?" she asked as she passed Megan.

"About the same. It's colder inside than it is outside."

"That's pretty cold," B.J. returned, shivering as her body welcomed the heat.

"How about a cup of coffee?" Megan asked, gesturing to the coffeepot that was always ready in the Randall kitchen.

"I'd love one, but I really came to talk to Pete."

"He's on his way, according to Brett. If you have time, you can wait for him. And I can have someone to talk to."

B.J. sat down at the table. "Come on, Megan. Things can't be that bad. Chad speaks to you, doesn't he?"

"Sure. He says, 'Could I have more coffee?' or 'Please pass the potatoes.'" She shoved her hand through her chin-length light brown hair.

"Didn't you explain to him that Janie didn't feel she should marry Pete until he loves her?"

"Of course I did. And he assured me Pete loves Janie. I suggested he tell Pete he loves her so they can make up and get married before the baby's born." Setting two cups of coffee on the table, she joined B.J. "Then he tells me Pete doesn't want to say those words."

B.J. shook her head. "These Randall men are something else. Sexy as can be and as hardheaded as mules. God must've put them on earth as punishment for women."

"Tell me about it," Megan agreed with a sigh, thinking of her own struggles getting Chad to admit his love for her.

The sound of several vehicles arriving distracted them.

"Are you expecting someone besides Pete?" B.J. asked. "If so, I can see him tomorrow. It's nothing urgent."

Before Megan could answer, Jake hurried into the kitchen, but he paused when he saw B.J. "I didn't know you were here."

His frown didn't make her feel welcome, but then Jake had never acted pleased with her presence.

"I'm just on my way out," she offered pleasantly, standing, hoping he'd never know how his attitude hurt her.

Megan intervened. "Don't be silly, B.J. You needed to talk to Pete. I'm sure this is him. Sit back down."

Before B.J. could move one way of the other, the door opened to Pete, Janie and her parents.

After the initial greetings, B.J. cornered Pete. "Call me tomorrow when you have a minute. I need to talk to you about our inoculation schedule. Good night, everyone."

"Wait, B.J." He turned to Janie. "Do you mind if we tell her?"

Janie smiled at her rather than at Pete. "Of course not. She's become a friend."

"Tell B.J. what?" Jake asked.

"Our news. We wanted to tell all of you at once," Pete added.

"Okay," Jake agreed. "Shall we adjourn to the living room? Megan, would you knock on Red's door and ask him to join us? I'll get Brett."

"I really don't have to stay, Janie, if you want it to be just family," B.J. whispered.

"Stay, please. We won't keep you long."

After her last visit to the Randall household, B.J. had vowed to avoid any more family gatherings. But she couldn't leave now. Curiosity had won out over common sense.

JAKE CALLED for Brett and hurried to the living room. He hoped Pete's news was good. He wanted his brothers married—but he also wanted them happy.

Chad had married Megan with everyone's approval. And all the Randalls loved Janie, too. But if she didn't want to be married to Pete, everyone would be unhappy.

"Janie and I have a couple of things to tell you," Pete began once everyone had arrived.

By the grin on his face and the fact that his arm was wrapped around Janie's shoulders, Jake assumed the news was good, that Pete and Janie had resolved their difficulties. Pete certainly looked happy, but Jake wasn't so sure about Janie.

"Janie has accepted my proposal. We're going to be married right away."

There was a lot of whooping and hollering from Brett and Chad, and Jake grinned. Chad was probably hoping his problems with Megan would be at an end.

Suddenly Jake remembered that Pete had said they had two announcements to make. "Pete, what's the second bit of news?"

Pete's grin widened even more, and Jake sighed in relief.

"The second announcement will really bowl you over, Jake. We're getting two for the price of one. Janie's having twins."

The celebration for his second announcement was even louder than the first. Jake let the others gather around Janie and Pete. He sat still, taking in the news, happiness bubbling up inside him. Two new Randalls. Two sets of little feet running around the house. And both of them before next Christmas.

Santa was coming to the Randalls. Yee-haw!

JANIE SUCKED IN her stomach as Megan tugged on the zipper. "I think we should've gotten a larger size. My waist is already starting to go."

"Nope. This one is perfect," Megan assured her as the zipper reached the top. "You're going to knock Pete off his feet."

"Didn't I already do that by having twins?" Janie asked ruefully.

B.J., her second bridesmaid, answered in place of Megan. "Maybe. But this will be a different kind of blow. You don't look anything like a cowgirl, Janie. More like a movie star."

Janie turned to look in the mirror. Her dark hair wasn't in its traditional braid. Instead, it flowed over her shoulders in shiny curls. The antique satin wedding gown with its matching veil gave her the look of a princess in a fairy tale, waiting for her prince to rescue her.

"I think I'm jealous," Megan suddenly said, gaining the attention of the other two.

"What are you talking about?" Janie asked anxiously. After all, she and Megan were about to become family.

"Chad and I got married on our own. I wore a blue suit. He wanted to come back home and have a traditional wedding, but I didn't want to wait. But you're so beautiful, and everyone's so excited, I think maybe I made the wrong choice."

Since Megan was grinning, neither of the other ladies took her seriously.

"It's how you feel when you wake the next morning that matters," B.J. said softly, her eyes clouding with memories.

Janie hoped the other two ladies couldn't read her mind, because her morning would be the same as all the other mornings without Pete, even if they were married.

By her choice.

I must be crazy, putting myself through such torture.

Jake had suggested she and Pete take the two-bedroom suite near Megan and Chad. Since Pete didn't want anyone to know they weren't a normal married couple, one room had been designated the babies' room, but Janie had suggested a daybed be rigged up like a sofa, filled with pillows, in case she had to spend nights with the babies after they were born.

Megan, who was in charge of redoing the house, agreed. While the room didn't have cribs yet, it had a sofa bed.

"It's time," Lavinia said, sticking her head in the door. "Brett's going to seat me now. Everything all right?"

"Everything's fine, Mom." Janie gave her mother her best smile, a little tremulous but warm. Her mother had worked nonstop the past four days to create the perfect wedding for her only daughter.

"Your father's waiting out here," Lavinia whispered before disappearing.

"Ready, Janie?" B.J. asked.

She nodded and faced the mirror one more time. Was she making a mistake? Could she ever make Pete love her?

Megan opened the door and waited for Janie to go to her father. Then Megan and B.J., dressed in amber taffeta, took their places. Janie stared after them as each marched down the aisle in the small church.

Though it was cold outside, the sun was streaming through the stained-glass windows, filling the church with rich colors.

The organ music swelled, and Janie realized her friends had reached the altar. Now it was her turn. She placed her hand on her father's arm and raised her gaze to his.

"You're beautiful, Janie, just like your mother," he whispered, and led her down the aisle.

PETE HAD FACED some dangerous situations in his life. The first time he'd ridden a bull, his insides had been all scrambled up *before* he'd gotten on the bull. But getting married was tougher.

Just when he thought he wouldn't last much longer, Janie, her hand tucked into her father's arm, appeared at the door to the chapel and took his breath away. He was suddenly glad Jake had insisted on a professional photographer. He didn't ever want to forget how beautiful Janie looked today.

There were a lot of things to worry about in this marriage, but today wasn't the time to concern himself with them. Now was the time to celebrate their union...and to celebrate the babies growing inside of Janie.

His babies.

"Dearly beloved, we are gathered here today to join this man and this woman in holy wedlock."

When Hank surrendered Janie's hand to Pete, he grasped it tightly, hoping Janie wouldn't realize how nervous he was. Then he looked into her bright blue eyes, and the fear that had been growing the past few hours left him. Everything would be all right.

Janie whispered her vows, her gaze pinned to Pete's strong features. He was a good man, even if he did have trouble loving her. She promised herself, even as she made her promises to Pete aloud, that she would find a way to make him love her.

When the pastor pronounced them husband and wife and suggested Pete kiss the bride, he did so with enthusiasm. So much enthusiasm, and so effectively, that Janie forgot they were in front of an audience. After all, he hadn't touched her since that kiss in front of the drugstore.

It occurred to Janie, as she enjoyed Pete's touch, she didn't have to hold back this once. She could kiss the boots off Pete if she wanted to, and he couldn't do much about it because they had an audience. With pleasure, she pressed against him, wrapping her arms around his neck, pretending, if only for a little while, that he loved her.

Pretending he loved her as much as she loved him.

Pretending happily-ever-after.

Only Jake's voice, reminding them they had a reception to go to, brought Janie back to reality. That and Pete's withdrawal. But she did feel some satisfaction when she saw the reluctance in his eyes.

Her cheeks bright red, she turned to face family and friends.

"Ladies and gentlemen," Jake announced, "it gives me great pleasure to introduce Mr. and Mrs. Peter Randall. I hope you'll all join us at the ranch for the reception."

Lavinia had wanted to have the reception at their house, but the Randalls' was so much larger, she'd agreed to Jake's offer. After all, most of the county would show up in spite of the short notice. She and Red, along with Mildred's help, had been baking nonstop.

Pete and Janie walked down the aisle, smiling at the well-wishers. Janie dreaded the drive to the ranch. She would be alone with Pete for the first time since they'd decided to marry. Life had been so hectic the past few days, she'd only seen him a few times, and always surrounded by people.

The photographer was waiting outside. "Give her a kiss, Pete, so I can get a good picture."

With a grin, Pete swept her to him, his lips covering hers. The man was incredible. Here they were in broad daylight, surrounded by a lot of people, and a warning that she wouldn't sleep with him, and she was longing for a double bed.

Thank goodness for the daybed in the babies' room.

"Janie," her mother called to her just as they started down the steps to Pete's truck.

"Yes, Mom?"

"Honey, I'm sorry, but we ran out of bedrooms. I hope you don't mind, but Great-Aunt Henrietta decided to make the trip after all, and there was nothing left."

A sense of foreboding came over Janie.

"Jake said she could sleep on that daybed you had put in your extra bedroom. It will just be for one night." Her mother looked at Pete, standing beside her. "I'm sorry, Pete. I know you'd prefer to be alone, but we don't have anywhere else to put her. You should have planned a real honeymoon."

"Remember? Janie didn't want one. But don't worry about Aunt Henrietta. We Randalls are a hospitable lot." His grin was wide enough to cover Wyoming, and Janie wanted to punch him in his breadbasket.

"Well, there's one good thing," Lavinia added with a wink. "Aunt Henrietta is as deaf as a fence post. She won't hear a thing."

Chapter Nine

"Wipe that grin off your face, Pete Randall," Janie ordered in frustration as soon as the two of them were in his truck.

"I'm not supposed to be happy on my wedding day?" he asked, his brown eyes wide with innocence.

"That's not why you were grinning and you know it. You think we're going to sleep together tonight because of Aunt Henrietta!"

"I always did like that lady," Pete returned, still smiling.

"You've never even met her!" Janie's great-aunt Henrietta lived in Cleveland, and Janie had seen her a few times as a child.

His sexy chuckle was the only response.

"Pete," Janie said in a warning tone.

"Relax, Janie. You know I'm teasing you. I gave you my word, didn't I? Whatever else you may think of me, you know I keep my promises."

Janie sighed and sank back against the seat. What Pete said was true. She knew he was a man of his word. In fact, the only thing she'd ever found to complain about him was the fact that he didn't love her.

She was more worried about her own reaction. Sleeping in the same bed with Pete would be a test of discipline she wasn't sure she'd pass.

"Did I tell you how beautiful you look today?" Pete asked softly, drawing her from her depressing thoughts.

The rush of warmth that filled her brought a blush to her cheeks. "No. But I don't think I look as good as you." Pete had worn a navy suit, a blue-and-gold tie and crisp white shirt. With his broad shoulders and narrow hips, he was every woman's dream.

"Honey, you're wrong about that. If we have little girls, I hope they both look like you."

For the first time since Doc's revelation, Janie considered the future. "It won't bother you if we have girls?"

He grinned. "Janie, I've been living in an all-man world for a long time. I'm looking forward to having a few women around, even if they're in diapers."

"You already have Megan and B.J. and her aunt. Soon the women will outnumber the men."

"Not likely," Pete objected with a grin. "B.J. and Mildred really aren't part of the family. They just live on the place. And since I don't think Jake will ever marry again, and Brett hasn't shown any inclination in that direction, either, we've got a long way to go before females outnumber males at the Randalls'."

Pete turned the truck onto the long driveway leading to the ranch, and the proximity of the ranch house reminded Janie of her original concern. "Pete, what are we going to do about this evening?"

"What do you mean?"

She sent him a disgusted look. "I'm talking about the sleeping arrangements, and you know it."

"We've got a king-size bed, Janie. Surely we can both sleep on it one night without any problems."

Sucking in her breath as she pictured Pete, his broad chest bare, wearing only his briefs as he slid under the covers within her reach, Janie shuddered. Could she keep her hands to herself? Could he?

When she said nothing, Pete pulled the truck to a halt by the house and turned her toward him. "I won't make love to you, Janie, unless you change your mind. But remember, you have a promise to keep, too." With those words, he leaned forward to kiss her. "We have an audience," he added just before his lips covered hers.

He extracted one hell of a down payment.

MEGAN STARED at Pete and Janie from the back door of the ranch house, remembering those first few minutes after her own marriage, just a couple of weeks ago. At least *she* had known her husband loved her.

Poor Janie.

"Remind you of us?" Chad whispered in her ear, his arm sliding around her.

"Not lately," she said coolly, hiding her reaction to his nearness.

Chad pulled her around to face him. "I think it's time we buried the hatchet, Meggie. I've missed you."

"But I didn't go anywhere, Chad. You're the one who withdrew because I didn't agree with you." She felt it was important to work out what went wrong, not sweep it under the rug.

"Hell, Meggie, you sided against Pete. What was I supposed to do?"

"Allow me to have my own opinion? I'm not an extension of you, Chad. I'm my own person. I love Pete like a brother, but that doesn't make him—or you—always right."

He linked his arms around her waist. "If I promise to do better, will you forgive me?"

How could she resist his smile? With a sigh of agreement, she melted against him and their lips met.

"Hey, you two, get out of the doorway," Red grumbled. "You're not the only newlyweds anymore."

"I don't know, Red. I'm feeling pretty much like a newlywed right now," Chad said, still holding Megan against him.

"I can tell, but I need some help."

Megan pulled from Chad's embrace. "What can I do?"

Mildred bustled into the kitchen in time to hear Megan's question. "Lavinia thinks you and B.J. should serve the punch and cake. You both look so pretty in your dresses."

"Thanks, Mildred. We were fortunate to find two alike." When she started toward the dining room, where the cake and punch were located, Chad followed. Over her shoulder, she said, "You should stay here and help Red."

"But who's gonna protect you from all those woman-hungry cowboys?"

Mildred chuckled, but Red ordered Chad to get the hot rolls from the oven before they burned.

"I could've done that," Mildred said, eyeing Red.

"Now, Miss Bates—" Red began.

"He's used to ordering me around, Mildred," Chad intervened. He'd noticed some tension between the two older people, though he didn't understand why. "You can put them in the bread basket Red has ready."

Mollified, Mildred picked up a spatula.

"Where are those two? I thought their truck arrived five minutes ago." Red frowned toward the back door.

"I think they got distracted," Chad offered, a big grin on his face. He had similar plans for his bride as soon as they could escape the celebration. In fact, he'd been doing a lot of thinking about babies, ever since he'd heard of Pete's approaching fatherhood.

Tonight might be a good time for a discussion with Meggie. Or something.

Janie and Pete entered the kitchen.

"It's about time," Red growled. Then, to everyone's surprise, he stepped forward and kissed Janie on the cheek. "Welcome to the family, Janie."

"Oh, Red, thank you!"

"Hey, watch it, Red," Pete protested, but the grin on his face told everyone he wasn't serious. "I'm not letting anyone kiss my bride but me."

"From what I saw out the back door, I'd say you've already used up your quota," Chad teased, laughing as Janie's cheeks flushed.

"Don't mind these men, child," Mildred said. "Pete, you take your beautiful bride in the living room and show her off. The house is full of people waiting to congratulate you." Then she turned to Chad. "You should join them, young man. Half the county is waiting to be introduced to your bride, too."

Chad willingly headed for the dining room. As he was leaving the kitchen, however, he wondered if it was safe to leave Red and Mildred alone.

"Who put you in charge?" Red growled behind him.

"I'm just trying to be helpful," Mildred returned.

Love might be brimming in the living room, Chad thought, but it was in short supply in the kitchen.

"FEEL FREE to go upstairs whenever you want," Jake said, pausing beside Pete. "You and Janie have been good sports, and no one would mind whenever you want to call it an evening."

"Thanks, Jake, but we're enjoying ourselves, right Janie?" Pete asked, slipping his arm around Janie's waist.

"Right," she murmured, struggling to summon a smile. It wasn't that she wasn't having fun. Sort of. She and Pete had been the center of attention for several hours. The food had been delicious, and the cutting of the wedding cake suddenly brought home to Janie that she'd actually achieved her dream of marrying Pete Randall.

But she was tired. And anxious about the coming night. Every time she thought of sharing a bed, even a king-size bed, with the sexy man next to her, she grew more and more nervous.

"How about a dance?" Pete asked, surprising Janie.

Jake stared at his brother, too. "You want to dance? There isn't much room in here with all the guests."

"Everyone can't dance, but we've got a guitar player and a fiddler here. Janie and I could have our dance, and you and B.J. and Chad and Megan can join us."

Even as he said it, Pete was motioning to a friend across the room. Within minutes, he had arranged a cleared space in the center of the room and the two musicians ready to play. He motioned for Chad and Megan to join them.

"Where's B.J.?" he called.

"Over here," she returned, waving to him. "Do you need something?"

"Pete, B.J. and I don't need to join in," Jake protested in a low voice.

Janie watched him curiously. He seemed agitated. She supposed he was afraid B.J. might get the wrong idea.

When B.J. reached their side and Pete explained what he wanted, she agreed, after a brief glance at Jake. The three couples gathered in the cleared space, and Pete nodded to the musicians.

Janie, after a moment of resistance, collapsed against Pete's chest. She was too tired to resist. His arms wrapped her against him, and they moved slowly to the music. With her eyes closed, she could almost imagine them alone six months ago, just beginning what she'd hoped would lead to a long life together.

Instead, it had led to a pregnancy and a marriage—in that order. And not because Pete loved her.

"You okay?" Pete asked, leaning down to whisper in her ear. He followed his question with a kiss beneath her ear, and she shivered against him.

"I'm a little tired," she murmured.

"I've kept you down here too long, I guess. But…I was enjoying pretending that our marriage is real. When we go upstairs, I have to face the fact that it's not."

Janie reared back from his hold. "Don't try to make me feel guilty, Pete Randall. It won't work."

"Darn, Janie Randall. You're too smart for me." His lips captured hers for a brief kiss. "By the way, I kissed Aunt Henrietta, too. I thought it was the least I could do to thank her."

"I don't know why you want to thank her. It's not going to change anything," she assured him, but she figured she was trying to convince herself as much as him.

"At least I'll get to see you when I wake up in the morning."

"I just hope the first thing you see isn't me bent over the toilet."

Pete frowned sharply. "You're getting sick? Did you call the doc?"

"It's only happened once."

"Wait a minute. I think he's still here. I'll—" Pete began, and started to leave her standing alone in the middle of the makeshift dance floor.

Janie grabbed him by his lapels. "Stop, Pete. I don't need you to find the doctor. I'm fine. Throwing up before a wedding is commonplace."

"Yeah, but Doc said—"

"Pete! For heaven's sake, it's no big deal." She wanted to shake him, but he was too big. The only things that got a response from the man were sex or babies.

"Have you been taking your vitamins?" he asked, still staring at her.

She rolled her eyes. "How romantic you are, Pete Randall."

"You want romance?" he asked, pulling her closer, his lips trailing down her neck.

Pulling back, she muttered, "That's sex, not romance."

"Hell, I already sent you flowers and candy. Much more romance, and I won't be able to pay for the babies," he teased.

"I don't need candy and flowers. And whatever else you do, don't help me with the grocery shopping, either," she ordered.

"You won't have to do any grocery shopping. Red takes care of that."

It suddenly struck Janie that her entire life had been turned upside down. "What am I going to do?"

"What do you mean?" Pete asked, frowning.

"Tomorrow. What am I going to do tomorrow?"

Pete seemed confused, and he stopped moving to the music. "What will you do tomorrow?" he repeated. "You'll relax, do whatever you want."

But Janie wasn't comforted. Suddenly she felt disoriented, lost.

"Janie, you don't have to do anything you don't want to. Your job is to take care of yourself and the babies." For the first time since he'd discovered she was pregnant, he reached down and pressed his hand against her stomach, his fingers splayed against the satin wedding gown.

"Pete!" Janie squealed softly. "People are watching."

He gathered her back into his arms. "We're married, Janie. They haven't forgotten even if you have."

She laid her head on his shoulder. "I'm so tired, I don't think I can even remember my name."

"Randall. You're a Randall, Janie Dawson Randall, and I think it's time I take you home." She didn't even protest when he swung her up into his arms and headed for the stairs.

"Wait!" Mildred called out as Pete passed her. "Janie hasn't thrown her bouquet!" She thrust the flowers, which had been resting on a nearby table, into Janie's hands.

"Make it fast, Mrs. Randall," Pete whispered. He climbed the first two stairs and turned her toward the living room.

"Put me down, Pete," she whispered.

"Nope. Toss that bouquet, little lady, and toss it fast."

Somehow, doing as her new husband ordered seemed the easiest thing at that moment. With one arm around his neck, she used the other to toss the bouquet over the balustrade.

Shrieks of laughter filled the air, and Janie looked down to discover a terror-stricken Brett clutching the bridal bouquet to his chest.

Pete didn't wait. He turned and headed up the stairs. Behind them, Janie heard Brett protesting.

"Hey! Wait! Throw it again, Janie. Not me! I wasn't supposed—"

"I think Janie did a fine job," Jake announced, and their guests burst into delighted laughter.

JAKE WATCHED Pete carrying Janie up the stairs. Before he could stop himself, he thought of doing the same to B.J. He'd have a harder time of it because she was a tall woman. Curvaceous.

He shook his head. What was he thinking? His first wife, Chloe, had been small, dainty, demanding. And he needed to remember that she was the reason he would never marry again.

The dance with B.J. had been more enjoyable than he'd expected. To fight the attraction he was feeling, he asked, "Are you sorry you didn't catch the bouquet?"

She looked at him, surprise on her face. "No, of course not, I'm not in the market for a husband." She chuckled as she looked across the room. "Though I can't say Brett thinks he is, either."

"He'll adjust. I've told him it's time he start looking around now that Pete's married."

"You're rather dictatorial about your brothers, aren't you?"

He frowned at her. "I'm the head of the family. It's up to me to see that they're all taken care of."

"Don't you think your brothers are old enough to figure things out for themselves?"

"No, I don't! And how I handle my family's business is none of yours." He regretted his burst of anger, knowing he should apologize, but he couldn't bring himself to do so.

After staring up at him in silence, she only said, quietly, "I think some of the guests are ready to leave now that Pete and Janie have gone upstairs. Perhaps you should go—"

"Yes. Thank you for reminding me of my duties." After giving a brief nod of his head, he strode to the door. Damn the woman. She always made him feel he'd been less than a gentleman.

"LOOKS LIKE WE'RE the last couple, Meggie," Chad whispered in her ear. "How about you? Are you exhausted?"

"It's been a busy few days," she said, smiling up at him. "But at least we're not angry with each other anymore."

"Yep. I've decided I've been pretty dense to waste even one day apart from you." He trailed kisses down the side of her face. "I think we may have more fun tonight than Pete and Janie."

"Do you think?" she asked, smiling at him.

"Yeah. And we could probably have triplets or quadruplets, if we tried, too." He closed his eyes and pulled her even closer.

Megan, surprised by his words, pulled away to look at his face. "What did you say?"

He smiled down at her. "I said we could— What's the matter? Don't you want to have kids?"

"Of course I do, Chad. But not right away. I'm going to redo the house with Adele, remember? Once I had a baby, I couldn't travel back to Denver or do all the work that's involved. You know that."

"Yeah, but I think our family is more important than a few couches."

He knew he'd made a mistake as soon as the words were out of his mouth, and Megan's glare confirmed his error.

"Is that what you think I do? Just buy a few couches? That interior decorating is one big shopping trip?"

"No, baby, I didn't mean that." Chad hurriedly retreated, whispering his words.

" 'Baby'? I don't like being called baby."

"Meggie, come on. We just made up."

She sniffed, her body stiff.

"Look, I was wrong to bring up the subject tonight. I know you've got important work to do. We'll talk about this stuff some other time." Hell, he might never bring up the subject again if it meant Megan would be angry with him. He regretted the past week's coldness between them.

Tonight he had plans to heat things up.

"Let's go upstairs, too. We'll leave the bachelors to say the good-nights for the Randalls."

Relief filled him when she agreed.

THE REMAINING RANDALLS, assisted by the Dawsons, bade the last of the guests goodbye and did a brief cleanup.

"Man, I forgot weddings were such an ordeal," Brett said, flopping down on the sofa.

"Get used to it. Yours is next," Jake said, a weary grin on his face.

"It seems to me you may be asking for trouble, Jake," Lavinia said as she joined Brett on the sofa.

"What do you mean, Lavinia? You think there's no woman out there insane enough to take on Brett?"

The others chuckled, as Jake intended, but Lavinia explained. "No. There's the possibility that your brothers will decide what's good for the gander is also good for the gander's older brother."

Jake pretended he didn't understand her slightly altered version of the old saying. "I don't think you've got that story right, Lavinia."

Brett leaned forward. "I think she does. Good idea, Lavinia. If marriage is such a great idea, why isn't Jake looking around?"

"Because I didn't catch the bouquet."

"That was an accident," Brett scoffed, his cheeks turning red. "It doesn't mean anything. You should be looking for your own woman, not one for me."

"How do you know I'm not? Mildred Bates was flirting with me tonight."

Again everyone laughed, except Red.

"Mildred is a very nice lady," Lavinia said, in spite of her laughter.

"Yes, she is. Only the nice ladies will do," Jake assured her.

"That wasn't what you called Chloe," Brett reminded him.

Jake wasn't pleased to have bad memories of his ex-wife brought up. "Fortunately there aren't too many women like Chloe around. By the way, the other day I heard she remarried."

"Poor guy," Brett muttered with an exaggerated shudder.

"You two are too hard on Chloe. It must've been difficult to move into this male bastion," Lavinia said.

Brett burst into laughter. "Too hard on Chloe? That's amusing, Lavinia. That's like saying one of Pete's bulls is just mischievous."

Though Lavinia smiled, tears filled her eyes as she said, "I think it may be hard for both Megan and Janie. You will be kind to Janie, won't you?"

While both Jake and Brett rushed to assure Lavinia that Janie would be treated well, Hank moved over and put his arm around his wife. "Don't worry, boys. Lavinia knows you'll be good to our Janie. She's just experiencing post-wedding blues. Everything's happened so fast, she's just realized Janie won't be going home with us."

Hank pulled Lavinia up from the couch. "Time for us to go home, sweetheart. At least Janie's close, and you can come see her whenever you want."

"Yes, of course. Sorry, Jake, Brett. We'll—we'll call tomorrow. Thanks for all your work, Red."

"Happy to do it, Lavinia."

After the Dawsons had driven away, Brett looked at the other two men. "I'm glad Hank knew what to do when Lavinia started crying. I sure didn't."

"Well, I hope you paid attention," Jake warned him, "because the Randalls include two ladies now. And it's up to us to keep them happy."

Brett looked up the stairs. "Naw, Jake. It's up to Pete and Chad to keep them happy. Speaking of which, I hope you remembered to have that discussion with them about the birds and the bees."

Chapter Ten

The door was open to their bedroom when Pete reached it with Janie in his arms. A good thing, he decided, since he thought Janie had gone to sleep on the way up the stairs.

He'd kept her at their reception too long, and he felt guilty because of it. She'd been tired an hour ago. But he'd loved holding her against him, kissing her to everyone's applause.

And he'd known when they came upstairs she would withdraw.

Her eyes fluttered open as he laid her down on the large bed. "Pete?"

"Hi, honey. We're home." His grin invited her to find the humor.

She rose up and looked around her, her bright blue eyes wide as they lit on several vases full of flowers.

"Megan and B.J. brought in the flowers. They said it made the room look more romantic." He hadn't told them the only thing the room needed was Janie for him to think it was romantic. "They also left the negligee as a gift."

Janie's eyes widened even farther as she looked over her shoulder to the other side of the bed. There, spread out in all its glory, was a silvery silk negligee, in material that would only cast a shadow over the wearer's charms.

"I—I can't wear that."

"Good."

"You don't like it?" she demanded, sitting straighter.

"Don't like it? Am I alive? Honey, any man would like to see his woman wearing something like that, especially if she looks like you." He paused, but she continued to stare at him, waiting for an explanation. "Unless he promised not to make love to her."

She dropped her gaze. "Oh."

"You haven't changed your mind, have you?"

His heart stopped beating while she considered her answer.

Then she whispered, "No."

"That's what I figured. So I hope you brought something a little less, uh, maybe I should say a little more . . . unsexy."

With a weary smile, she stood. "I did. Are—are my bags here?"

He pointed them out beside the closet door. "Just get out what you need tonight. You can unpack tomorrow, after you've rested. I'm going down for a late-night snack while you get ready for bed." The relief on her face didn't make him feel good, but he tried to ignore his disappointment. "Don't wait up for me."

She nodded, avoiding his gaze.

Pete stepped out of the room, pulling the door closed behind him. Then he collapsed against it and breathed deeply.

Man, keeping his hands off Janie was going to be tough. Especially when she slept in his bed. He'd better stay gone until she'd fallen asleep. With a sigh, he loosened his tie, took off his coat to hang it on the doorknob, shoved his hands in his pants pockets and strolled to the stairs.

Hearing voices still in the living room, he came to an abrupt halt. Hell, he'd completely forgotten that everyone else hadn't gone to bed already. Now what was he going to do?

Every bedroom in the house was filled with guests spending the night. His old bedroom was off-limits. Their second room was filled with Great-Aunt Henrietta.

As he stood there thinking, he heard someone near the bottom of the stairs say, "I think we'll go on up to bed, now, Jake. We're too old for such late-night shenanigans."

Pete didn't know who was speaking, and it didn't matter. He didn't want *anyone* to see him lingering in the hall on his wedding night. He sprinted back to his bedroom door. Grabbing his jacket, he opened the door, slipped in and quietly shut it behind him.

Then he turned around in time to discover Janie coming out of the bathroom wrapped in a towel. A very brief towel.

"Pete!" she gasped.

"Janie!" he yelped at the same time.

She backed toward the bathroom, clasping the towel tightly around her. "I thought you wouldn't be back yet."

"I wasn't— I didn't mean to— I couldn't get to the kitchen without everyone downstairs seeing me. I didn't want them to know—"

She interrupted him, her cheeks red. "I'm through in the bathroom if you need it. My pajamas are in here."

He edged his way past, avoiding touching her, but he couldn't keep his gaze from tracing every inch of her pale flesh. He was panting by the time he closed the door behind him.

Deciding a shower was in order, he turned on the water, all cold, and stripped down. When he finally dried off a few minutes later, he felt a little more in control. As long as the door was closed.

When he finally got up the nerve to open the bathroom door, he discovered only a small lamp burning on his side of the big bed. Janie was curled into a tight little ball on the other side, almost falling off the edge.

"Janie?" he whispered.

No answer. Could she already be asleep? It would make life easier for him if she was. He crept over to gaze down at her beautiful face, pale with exhaustion but relaxed in sleep.

He reached down to caress her cheek, longing filling him. The desire to hold her against him, to protect her, to love her, filled him. Groaning, he stepped back and rounded the bed. Lifting the cover, he got in and pulled the blankets to his chin.

After several minutes of trying to ignore Janie's presence, he made a decision.

He'd promised not to make love to her. But he hadn't promised not to hold her. Turning, he reached out and slid her next to him. Though he feared she would awaken, he was delighted when she cuddled against him, her eyes closed.

With a sigh, he shut his eyes, too. He was tired. But he loved the feel of her against him. And, in spite of his promise, he was experiencing something new on his wedding night. He would wake up in the morning next to Janie.

Not a bad way to start the day.

JANIE WOKE the next morning slowly. *Must've turned off the alarm.* She struggled to open her eyes. When she did finally manage that simple task, she stared around her, the events of the past day slowly reinstating themselves.

She was pregnant.

She was married.

She'd shared the bed with Pete.

At that thought, her head whipped around to be sure she was alone. During their affair, they'd never spent an entire night together.

With a mixture of disappointment and relief, she discovered Pete was nowhere to be seen. She relaxed against the pillow... until she realized her pillow was in the middle of the bed. She distinctly recalled clutching the side of the bed last night.

The indentation in the pillow next to hers showed Pete hadn't sought the far reaches of the big bed, either. Had they spent the night together wrapped in each other's arms . . . and she'd missed it?

She groaned and swung back the covers. No use thinking about such a thing. It couldn't happen again. As soon as the other room was abandoned, she'd move in. Discreetly, of course, as she'd promised Pete, but she couldn't risk the temptation of sleeping with him again.

Fortunately her stomach seemed settled this morning. She set about getting ready to face the world, including her new family.

When she started down the stairs, the nervous tension in her stomach surprised her. She'd known the Randalls all her life. But things were different this morning.

Red stood by the sink and Megan sat at the table, working on a sketch, when Janie entered the kitchen. "Good morning."

Megan smiled and Red rushed to her side to take her arm as if she were unstable. "Here, Janie, come sit down," he urged.

She looked at him in surprise.

Megan chuckled. "You didn't know you'd suddenly become an invalid, did you?"

"Now, Megan, don't go talkin' that way," Red ordered. "We're just tryin' to be careful."

"About what?" Janie asked, still puzzled.

"Why, about you and the babies. Pete warned us all this morning."

"Pete warned you about what?" Janie asked.

They'd reached the table, and Janie sat down across from Megan as she asked her question. Red didn't answer, because he was hurrying across the room to the stove.

"Now, Janie, do you want eggs and bacon with flapjacks, or—?"

"Red, it's ten o'clock. Lunch is in two hours. All I need is a piece of toast, a cup of coffee and, I suppose, a glass of milk."

"But Pete said—"

"Yes, what exactly did Pete say?" she demanded, irritation building in her.

"That we were to take care of you," Megan explained. "He laid down the law to all of us that you weren't to lift a finger, and we were to feed you every time your mouth opened." Her grin told Janie she would understand her reaction.

Janie shook her head, a rueful smile on her face. "Red, just toast, coffee and milk."

"Are you sure you should have coffee? I read—"

"One cup won't hurt me."

"But Pete—"

Janie got up from the table and crossed to the coffeepot, reaching for the mugs stored just above it.

"I coulda done that, Janie," Red insisted.

On the way back to the table, she kissed his cheek. "I know, Red, but I'm not an invalid, in spite of Pete's warnings. But I will let you fix me some toast, just this once."

Though Red grumbled under his breath, he set about fixing her toast, and Janie sat back down across from Megan.

"I'm going to have problems here, aren't I?"

"Only if you want to do anything except breathe," Megan agreed. "The Randall men aren't used to having women around, much less a pregnant one. Pete envisions keeping you seated on a satin pillow, being waited on hand and foot, until the babies are born."

"I'd go out of my mind."

Megan nodded in sympathy.

Red brought over the toast and a glass of milk before refilling his own coffee cup and joining them at the table. "Anything else I can get for you? Megan, you need more coffee?"

"No, Red, thanks. Besides, I'm not pregnant. I can get my own coffee." Megan's grin took the sting out of her words.

"As far as I know, being pregnant hasn't impaired my legs, either," Janie protested.

"Now, Janie, don't get all hot and bothered. Pete just wants to take care of you because of...well, past history," Red said, and then looked alarmed.

"I suppose he warned you not to talk about my mother's problems...or his mother's? Does he think I don't know?" Janie stared at the other two in disgust.

"He doesn't want you to dwell on bad things," Megan assured her.

Again Janie rolled her eyes. "I'm surprised he even let me out of bed."

"Oh!" Red jumped up as if something had bitten him. "I forgot. He left you a note in case you got up before he got back." He hurried across the kitchen to the desk where he stored everything from recipes to receipts. He returned to hand Janie a folded piece of paper.

> Prop your feet up and take it easy. Red will get you whatever you want.
>
> Pete

Janie folded the paper and put it in her jeans pocket. Not exactly romantic, but she hadn't had too many notes from Pete. Unconsciously she sighed after sipping her coffee.

"Bad news?" Megan asked.

"No. Just orders to do nothing."

"You should give yourself time to adjust. You've had several big changes in your life recently."

"And that's exactly the reason I need something to keep me from going crazy. I've never sat around the house my entire life."

"You could watch some movies," Red suggested, "or read. The boys have lots of books around."

"Thanks, Red, but I'm talking about more than just today. I'm going to be pregnant for the next seven months. If all I do is sit around, I'll be as big as a house."

With a grin, Red said, "I reckon you'll get big as a house no matter what you do."

"Thanks for that depressing thought," she returned, but she was smiling.

"Want to walk down to the horse barn with me?" Megan suggested. "I love to check on the babies."

"Great! I haven't seen the latest foals. I'll go get my coat."

"I'll get it for you," Red offered, leaping to his feet.

Janie, already standing, stared at him. "Don't be ridiculous, Red. I haven't broken a leg." Then she rushed out the kitchen door.

"Tell that to Pete," Megan suggested, sharing a wry grin with Red.

NORMALLY PETE ENJOYED his time in the saddle, especially on a day like today, when, in spite of the cold, the sun shone and the wind was still. But today, all he could think about was Janie.

Had she gotten up yet? He'd debated staying in bed, holding her until she opened her eyes. Then he'd realized that might not be such a good idea. She might feel he hadn't stuck to his part of the bargain. Or that he was trying to tempt her into dissolving that agreement.

And that would be true.

But he worried that she might throw up this morning and not tell him or the doctor. She'd gotten irritated with him last night when he'd tried to find Doc Jacoby.

And what if she didn't take her vitamins? He'd forgotten to remind her in the note he'd left. She and the babies were his responsibilities now. He needed to take good care of them.

"You okay?" Jake asked, riding up to his side.

"Yeah. Fine."

"We're almost back to the corral. Why don't you make sure the gate is open and then go on up to the house? You probably want to check on Janie."

Pete gave him a grateful smile and nudged his horse to a lope. Jake was almost as anxious about Janie and the babies as he was.

His anticipation grew as he reached the house. The thought of seeing Janie again filled him with all kinds of emotions. "Hi, Red," he said as he rushed through the kitchen, heading for the stairs.

"Hey, Pete, where you going?"

"To check on Janie. Has she come downstairs this morning?"

"Yeah. She and Megan walked to the horse barn."

Pete came to a sudden halt, a ferocious frown on his brow. "What did you say?"

"She and Megan walked—"

"You let her go outside?" Pete demanded, slowly walking toward Red.

"How was I supposed to stop her?"

"She might catch cold," Pete said as he changed directions and sped toward the back door. "You should've told her to go lie down and rest."

By the time he reached the horse barn, he was muttering under his breath, so that little puffs of chilled air followed his progress. He should've known better than to leave Janie there on her own.

Throwing open the door, he roared, "Janie? Where are you?"

"Shh," Megan cautioned, leaning against the half door of one of the birthing stalls.

Automatically Pete lowered his voice. "Where's Janie?"

"Here, helping B.J.," Megan whispered as Pete drew closer.

"What?" Pete exclaimed hoarsely as he rushed to Megan's side.

The two women in the stall were concentrating on the mare and the just-born foal.

"Thanks, Janie. You were a lot of help," B.J. said as she and Janie helped the newborn to its feet.

"No problem. It was a pleasure to watch you work, B.J."

"Janie, are you crazy?" Pete demanded, steel in his voice.

His wife—he liked the thought of that word— wheeled to stare at him. "What's the matter, Pete?"

"Have you forgotten you're pregnant?"

Janie's hand stole to her stomach, still relatively flat. "No, I don't think so."

"You should be in the house, resting. You might hurt yourself helping B.J. Or you might catch cold."

"Or I might be struck by a falling meteor. What's your point, Pete?"

B.J. intervened. "Pete, I wouldn't let Janie do anything that would endanger the babies. But an extra pair of hands helped."

Pete stared at all three women in frustration. They didn't understand. "Come on, Janie. Get cleaned up, and I'll take you back to the house."

"You think I can't find it on my own?" She hadn't moved.

"No, but you might decide to stop and pitch a few bales of hay up to the barn loft. Or brand a few cows. Or round up the strays, for all I know." His frustration edged his voice.

Janie wanted to let her temper loose, to tell Pete what he could do with his coddling, but she couldn't. Not in front of the other two women. And not to Pete. As much as his concerns drove her crazy, she couldn't jump all over him. "I'll come with you, Pete, but we're going to have to talk."

"Sure, Janie, once you're inside and warm."

"Pete, it's not that cold in here." She couldn't help but protest. The man acted as if they were wandering around in a blizzard.

He stood patiently waiting.

Rolling her eyes at the other two women, she bade them goodbye and left the stall, crossing to the sink to wash up. Then she put her jacket on, with Pete's help, of course, and the two of them left the barn.

"Pete, I'm not made of Venetian glass. I won't break into a million pieces."

"I'm just trying to take care of you, Janie. You're my responsibility now. I don't want you or the babies to get hurt."

His responsibility. That wasn't what she wanted to be. She wanted to be the love of his life. His partner. Instead, she was his responsibility. "That's sweet of you, Pete, but millions of women are pregnant all the time. They still manage to get some work done."

"There's no need for you to work. Red takes care of the house, and we take care of the ranch. All you have to do is take care of the babies."

Janie came to a halt in the snow. "So for the next seven months, you expect me to sit and contemplate my navel as it expands to the size of a blimp?"

Pete blinked several times. "A blimp? Are you going to get that big?"

"Pete Randall! Quit trying to distract me. You know what I'm trying to say."

"Yeah, I do, honey," he assured her, a warm smile on his face that reassured her even as it frustrated her. His arm came around her shoulders, and he urged her on toward the house.

"Well? I have to have something to do, or I'll go crazy. Megan is working on redoing the house. Red doesn't really need any help. What am I going to do with myself?"

"I don't know. We'll figure out something." He brushed his cold lips against hers, and Janie fought to keep her desire under control. This man could start a fire inside her in the coldest temperatures.

"Hey, Pete, Janie," Brett called as he made his way to the house. "Some honeymoon you two are having. You should go away to Hawaii or somewhere."

Pete and Janie, having reached the porch, stood waiting for Brett to join them. "Maybe we will take a honeymoon, but it might be a good idea to go after the babies are born."

Janie wanted to sock her new husband. He thought it would be easy to leave newborn twins? He had no idea how his life would change once the babies were born.

"I wish I had something like that to look forward to. I've got so much paperwork stacked up that I'll never get finished, even if I don't ride out this afternoon. And Jake needs me in the saddle."

Like a light bulb in the comic strips, an idea jumped into Janie's head. "I can help you with the paperwork, Brett, if you'll show me how you have things set up."

The rising pleasure on Brett's face died a quick death as Pete roared, "No!"

Chapter Eleven

"Pete, what's the matter with you?" Janie demanded, her hands on her hips.

"Don't you recognize the signs?" Brett asked, a comical look on his face. "I think he's about to blow."

"That's enough, little brother. You can do your own paperwork. I'm not having Janie worrying about all that stuff." Pete grabbed Janie's arm and tugged her toward the door.

"Pete Randall, I've just about had it!" Janie protested, pulling away from him. "You're acting like I'm a mummy, wrapped up and standing in a museum. I'm going to go crazy if I don't have something to do."

"Janie—" Brett began.

"You stay out of this, Brett," Pete ordered.

"*I* want to talk to Brett."

"You—"

"What's going on?" Jake asked, having walked up to the porch without the other three noticing.

All three tried to explain the discussion.

Jake held up a hand. "Can't we talk about it inside? I'm cold and hungry."

Janie suddenly exploded. "No, *we* can't! I may have married one Randall, but I didn't marry all four!" Then she threw open the door and stomped through the kitchen, ignoring Red's cheerful greeting. She didn't stop until she reached the bedroom she'd shared with Pete last night.

The sight of the freshly made bed enraged her even more. In the hour she'd spent in the barn, Red had rushed upstairs to tidy up after her. Her mother would be ashamed of her.

And she could admit to herself, behind the closed door, that she felt like a guest at an expensive hotel.

But she wanted to feel like family.

"Janie?" Pete called softly, rapping on the door.

She tried to ignore him. But she couldn't. She'd already been more than rude. Reluctantly she opened the door.

"Janie, Jake didn't mean to interfere. We're all wanting to do what will make you happy."

"I apologize."

Pete's smile replaced the anxious expression on his face. "Good. Lunch is ready."

"I'm not hungry. I think I'll lie down for a while."

Her simple words immediately triggered Pete's overprotective urges. "Should I call Doc? What can I get you? Do you need anything? I'll bring a tray—"

"Pete!" Janie almost shouted, grabbing him by both arms. "I'm sulking! Okay? That's all I'm doing. Go eat your lunch and ignore me."

She stepped back and closed the door in his face.

Pete stared at the piece of wood that separated him from his wife, stunned by her words and her action. What did he do now?

He'd fix a tray for her, of course. She couldn't be allowed to skip meals. That wouldn't be good for her or the babies. Damn! He'd still forgotten to ask about morning sickness and her vitamins.

His mind filled with concern about Janie, he didn't remember that he had to face his family until he opened the kitchen door to discover them waiting at the table, all their gazes fixed on his face.

"Oh. Sorry I kept you waiting," he muttered, and sat down in his usual seat, ignoring the place set for Janie.

"Where's Janie?" Jake asked sharply.

"She decided to rest. I'll take a tray up to her before I go out again."

Megan leaned across the table. "Do you want me to check on her?"

"Should we call the doctor?" Brett asked.

"Is she mad at me?" Jake demanded, a frown on his brow.

Chad's hand reached for Megan's, as if talk of Janie's health made him appreciate his wife beside him.

Pete felt envy fill his heart. He wished he could claim Janie as simply. "No. No, she assured me she's fine."

After Red served the meal and they all began eating, Pete asked Megan quietly, "Did Janie get sick this morning? I mean, throw up?"

Megan's eyebrows arched. "She didn't mention it if she did."

"Did she take her vitamins?"

Shaking her head, Megan said, "I didn't see her take them, but Janie is an adult. And I'm sure she'd do whatever she needs to take care of the babies."

Janie might seem like an adult to Megan, but Pete had been keeping an eye on her all her life. Somehow he'd always felt responsible for her. And now that he'd gotten her pregnant, the feeling had only increased. "I'll check with her later," he muttered, unwilling to show how anxious he was.

"She probably just needs to rest," Jake assured him. "I've heard pregnant women need a lot of rest."

Brett raised his head and stared at his oldest brother. "You've heard?"

One would've thought Brett had questioned his sanity. Jake stiffened and stared down his little brother. "Yes, I've heard. You got a problem with that?"

Shrugging, Brett looked away. "Nope. I just never pictured you standing around talking about pregnant women."

"I don't, damn it!" Then, as if confessing a terrible sin, he muttered, "I bought a book."

Pete's eyes widened, and he felt incredibly stupid. Why hadn't he thought of that? Here he was the father, totally inexperienced in these things, and his brother had bought a book. "Reckon I could borrow it?" he asked Jake, a smile on his face to show his appreciation.

"Sure. You want to stay in this afternoon and read it?"

Nothing else could've shown Pete how supportive Jake was trying to be. They were shorthanded today because several of the cowboys had the flu. He knew Jake needed him in the saddle. He shook his head. "No, thanks. I'll read it this evening. I'll be down to the barn as soon as I take Janie some food."

"Um, Pete, why don't I take Janie a tray? She can eat and then take a nap so she'll feel better when you come in this evening."

Pete thought of Janie's temper and decided Megan was right. "Thanks, I'd appreciate that."

"Well, ready to be on our way, then?" Jake asked, standing.

As they moved to the door, after thanking Red, Chad leaned over to Pete and whispered, "After you finish that book, do you think I could borrow it?"

Both men looked over their shoulders to make sure Megan didn't overhear them. Pete nodded his agreement.

Brett, behind them, saw no need for secrecy. "Damn! After Chad, I guess I'm going to have to read it. And I'm not even married yet!"

JANIE PLACED HER EAR against the door. No sound. Softly, she rapped on the wood. Nothing. She reached down to turn the knob but stopped when knocking sounded.

It took her a second to realize the knocking was coming from the door to the bedroom, not the bathroom door leading into their second room. She hurried back through the bathroom to open the door, steeling herself to face Pete again.

Instead, she discovered Megan. Carrying a tray.

"Megan! What are you doing?"

"Bringing you some lunch. Pete was going to, but I offered."

Janie took the tray from Megan and stood back so she could enter the bedroom. "I'm ashamed of myself. I would've come down if I got hungry. There's no need to wait on me."

"I know that," Megan assured her, a smile on her face, "but you just got married yesterday. A little pampering won't hurt you."

Janie didn't know why such behavior was easier to accept from Megan than Pete, but it was.

"Would you like to come in and keep me company? Or I could go back down to the kitchen...." She trailed off, watching Megan.

"I'd love to keep you company. Do you want to get into bed to eat?"

"No. In fact, I was just thinking about unpacking. Has Great-Aunt Henrietta been downstairs yet? I didn't see her earlier." Janie set the tray on the bed and uncovered the steaming bowl of stew, the tossed salad and crisp rolls. "This smells delicious."

"Your mom and dad picked up your great-aunt and the couple from Denver and took them all to the airport this morning. Sorry I forgot to mention it earlier. Your great-aunt didn't want to be gone too long because of her cats. She said to tell you goodbye."

"Oh, thanks." At least she knew she wouldn't have to face another night in Pete's arms. She ignored the disappointment that filled her.

After she'd taken several bites, she looked at Megan. "I guess I owe everyone an apology. I'm usually not such a prima donna."

"Of course you aren't. These Randall men are a difficult lot. But they really only want to take care of you. Jake even bought a book."

Janie stared at her. "What? A book about what?"

"Pregnancy, silly!" Megan assured her with a chuckle. "Can't you picture Jake hiding in the barn reading a book about pregnant women instead of some girlie magazine? He admitted it at lunch, and I had a hard time not laughing."

"Jake?" Janie squeaked in surprise.

"Yes, and Pete's going to borrow it."

Janie joined Megan in some cleansing laughter.

The men returned at dark, cold, tired and hungry. But it cheered Pete to find Janie in the kitchen with Megan and Red, setting the table for dinner.

"You've got twenty minutes to clean up," she announced as they entered, smiling at all of them.

Pete wanted her smile just for him. He moved toward her, his gaze intense. Her eyes widened, but she didn't sidestep his embrace. "Hi, honey. I'm home," he whispered in her ear before he kissed her.

When he released her, he had to fight the desire to scoop her up in his arms and continue upstairs.

"You smell like horse," she complained, but she wouldn't meet his gaze. "Go grab a shower before we eat."

"Care to come scrub my back?"

"Pete!" Her reddened cheeks delighted him. He much preferred this homecoming to the one at lunch.

"We've got everything under control down here," Red added, his eyes twinkling. "Just don't take too long, or we'll eat without you."

"Newlyweds!" Brett exclaimed. Since Chad and Megan had already left the room, his complaint fell only on Pete and Janie.

"Jealous, little brother?" Jake asked. "If so, I know a remedy."

"Don't start, Jake. You've got Pete and Chad married. You should be satisfied." Brett started to the kitchen door, hoping to escape his big brother's attention.

"It's only a matter of time," Jake shouted after him as he followed him out of the kitchen.

"Skedaddle," Red insisted, moving around Pete and Janie. "I'm not letting my food go cold. Twenty minutes flat, no more, no less."

"I should stay and help—" Janie began.

"Nope. *Newlyweds* should go up together," Pete insisted, hoping she caught his message. After all, she'd promised to keep the state of their marriage a secret.

After staring at him intently, she turned without a word and headed for the stairs. When they arrived at their bedroom, he reached in front of her and opened the door. "After you, Mrs. Randall."

She entered ahead of him but then stood awkwardly in the center of the room.

Pete looked around, too. "You unpacked? You didn't overdo it, did you? Red or I could've helped you."

"No. I didn't need any help. And Red has enough to do."

Pete grunted as he began unbuttoning his shirt and headed for the closet for a fresh one. He'd carefully left half the closet space for Janie when he'd moved his things in. Somehow, their clothes sharing a space, even if he and his wife didn't, sent a thrill up his spine. He pushed back the closet door to discover the space inside didn't look any different than it had yesterday.

"Where are your things?" he asked, wheeling around to face her.

"In the other room," she said quietly, meeting his look.

He strode through the bathroom to the other bedroom, over to the closet and threw the door open. He stood there, staring at rows of shirts, skirts and dresses, feminine clothing, hanging pristinely in the closet.

She couldn't even share the closet?

Frustration rose up in him, and he reached forward and filled his big hands with hangers. Before Janie could protest, he had spun around, his hands grasping her clothes, and headed back to the other room.

"Pete, what are you doing?"

He ignored her.

"Pete, where are you going with my things? We're not sharing the same room, remember?" She tried to get between him and the closet door, but he wouldn't let her.

"Janie," he said softly, slowly, emphatically, "we may not be sharing the same bed, at least not now, but we sure as hell are going to share the same closet. Don't argue with me." His order didn't sit well with her, he could tell, but she stepped back, frowning at him.

He made a second trip. When he came back into the bedroom, she hadn't moved. But she spoke. "All my things won't fit in the closet."

"Then we'll *both* keep things in the other closet. But when Red puts our clean clothes away, I don't want him getting any ideas."

"But, Pete, I told Red I'd take care of our rooms. And our laundry. No one will know."

"I'll know," he insisted, whirling around to glare at her. "We're married, Janie. Get used to it."

Without waiting for an answer, an answer he feared he wouldn't like, Pete slammed shut the closet door and strode into the bathroom, closing the door behind him. Ripping off his shirt, he sat on the side of the tub and pulled off his boots, then shed the rest of his clothing.

The tension didn't dissolve even a little until steaming hot water splayed on his broad shoulders. But the water massage couldn't dissolve the raging hunger inside him. He wanted Janie so badly he could hardly concentrate.

But it wasn't just sex that fueled that hunger. He wanted her to be a part of him, emotionally as well as physically. He wanted the right to claim her. The wedding should have given him that right. But he knew, if no one else did, that Janie had only married him because of the babies. She'd made it clear she never would've walked down that aisle if Doc hadn't told her she was having twins.

A jarring thought brought him up short. Wasn't it the same for him? He wouldn't have married her if she weren't pregnant. After all, he'd refused her proposal before he'd known. What had changed suddenly? Pete refused to contemplate how his feelings for Janie had changed. There was too much else to think about. Like what would happen once the babies were born. Janie couldn't leave, could she? Taking his children with her? Such a thought almost stopped his heartbeat. Why hadn't he thought of it before?

Because he'd wanted to believe that once they were married, everything would work itself out.

So far, that hadn't happened.

He savagely shut off the tap and stepped from the shower, grabbing a towel from the linen closet. He rubbed himself vigorously, hoping to restore his belief in their future...together.

Then he swung open the bedroom door and discovered his wife sitting on the bed, staring at him as he stood in the doorway stark naked.

AFTER DINNER THAT NIGHT, Pete challenged Chad and Megan to a game of pool. He didn't want Janie to retreat to ''her'' room, locked away from his sight.

"Hey, good idea," Chad agreed. He took Megan's hand and led her toward the room that housed their pool table.

Pete kept his gaze on their locked hands, envy filling him. Every time he touched Janie, she pulled away. Maybe he could coach her on her playing.

Minutes later, after Chad racked the balls, Pete knew he'd have a better shot of getting Janie to coach him. They hadn't played together since she was eleven or twelve. Somewhere along the way, she'd improved her game. Not to mention a few other things.

Chad leaned over to kiss his wife. "Sorry, darlin', but I may have to trade you in for Janie. Especially if we ever get challenged by someone other than family."

Megan puffed up in pretend anger. "Only married a couple of weeks and you're already tired of me?"

Chad dropped his pool cue with no compunction and wrapped his arms around Megan. "Changed my mind," he assured her, burying his lips in her hair.

"Your shot, Megan," Pete said, hoping to bring the attention back to the game. Otherwise, he was going to die of frustration. "Good playing, Janie."

Chad picked up his cue stick and patted Megan on her rear. "Go get 'em, tiger."

"Behave, Chad, or Janie and Pete won't play with us again," Megan warned him, and then turned her attention toward the table.

A puzzled frown came over her face. "What do I do?"

Before either man could offer advice, Janie began explaining Megan's options and showing her how to shoot.

Chad stepped over to Pete. "Remember Rita? When I offered to help Megan when the two of you were playing us, she became enraged. She didn't want to lose."

Pete remembered. Rita was the third decorator who'd visited the ranch with Megan and Adele. Once she'd caught sight of the Randall brothers, though, her mind was on activities other than decorating. She hadn't been their kind. Like Megan. And Janie.

Janie bent over the table to demonstrate a shot for Megan, and his gaze unerringly traced her trim shape. Beautiful and kind. Smart. And hardheaded as all get-out. He grinned. When he'd come out of the bathroom, she'd looked her fill. And then opened the dresser drawer to toss him a pair of briefs. "You'd better hurry before dinner starts." Then she'd left the room.

He didn't think he could've mustered such sang-froid if Janie had been naked. In fact, even thinking about such a sight had his blood surging.

"Your shot, Pete," Janie called to him.

Surprised, he looked at the others. "Um, I think I need some help, too. Like Megan."

Chad stepped forward.

"Not you, bozo," Pete growled, and then smiled sweetly at Janie.

"Get real, Pete. You were an expert by the time I was born," Janie replied, lifting an eyebrow.

"Well, then, how about a good-luck kiss?"

To his surprise, she stepped forward and brushed her lips across his, one hand resting on his chest for balance. His immediate fantasy of taking her right there on the pool table didn't help his aim. He missed.

"I think Pete's trying to make me not feel so bad," Megan said, smiling at her brother-in-law.

Chad chuckled. "I think Pete's mind isn't on the game. And if Janie kisses him for luck every time it's his turn, we'll win."

"Maybe Megan will return the favor and do a little distracting of her own," Pete suggested, wrapping an arm around Janie's slim figure. His heart clutched when she leaned her head against his chest, her silky hair resting against his chin.

"Not a bad idea. I'll prove I can handle distraction better than you," Chad assured his brother. Then he pulled Megan to him and kissed her thoroughly. Casually he released her and bent over the table. And missed.

"Damn! Unlucky shot," he muttered, avoiding his brother's gaze.

Janie stepped up to the table for her turn.

"Wait a minute! She's been doing better than all of us. Give her a kiss, Pete. Let's see if she can handle distraction better than the rest of us." Chad grinned at both of them before he ordered, "And no lily-livered peck like the last one."

Pete eyed his wife, wondering if she'd protest. When she turned toward him expectantly, he took her response as a green light. And proceeded with great expertise. And a lot of heat.

"Wow!" Chad said as Pete released Janie. "Janie, if you can make a shot after that, you've got ice water in your veins."

Pete thought so, too. He knew he was on fire.

Janie stepped up to the table and studied the balls' positions. Pete looked for any flicker of distraction or lack of concentration. It seemed important to him that Janie be as distracted as he was. As if it would be proof that his wife cared for him, wanted him.

She lined up her shot, pushed her long black braid back over her shoulder and hit the cue ball.

Pete stared in dismay as the little white ball rolled across the table, smacked into the nine ball and drove it into the hole.

Perfect shot.

Chapter Twelve

When their heavy breathing returned to normal, and Chad lay relaxed with Megan wrapped in his arms, she whispered, "Do Janie and Pete strike you odd in any way?"

Chad frowned and raised his head slightly. "What are you talking about?"

"They don't seem . . . comfortable with each other. Janie even avoids Pete's touch. And he seems reluctant."

"You must've had your eyes closed when he kissed her before she made that last shot." As if the memory reminded him of what he liked, too, he kissed his wife again. "Mmm, but I like kissing now better than kissing while playing pool."

"Me, too, but—"

"Give 'em a break, sweetheart. They've only been married a day or two. Unlike us. We've been married two weeks tomorrow. We're old hands at this sort of thing." He kissed her again. "But don't you worry about old Pete. He'll kiss Janie off her feet in no time." He chuckled. "Silly remark, I guess, since she's already pregnant."

Megan lay pressed against her husband's heart, well satisfied with her lot in life. But she also still had doubts about Pete and Janie. She didn't want anything to be wrong, but she couldn't quell the feeling that something wasn't right.

But she wasn't going to say any more to her husband about it.

"In fact," Chad whispered, running a hand up and down her back, "we may have been married first, but Pete's one up on me. Or should I say two up?" he added with a chuckle. "Maybe we'd better practice again."

"This isn't a competition," Megan protested but weakly. She was enjoying his suggestion too much.

WHEN JANIE WOKE the next morning, she didn't have any trouble remembering where she was. She was in another room, away from Pete, in a single bed, missing his warmth and touch.

The sound of the shower immediately filled her with the picture of Pete when he'd opened the door yesterday sans his clothes. It had been all she could do to speak straight. Then she'd had to play pool with the man, in front of Chad and Megan, and try to ignore her hormones.

No one had been more surprised than her when she'd sunk the nine ball. Especially since she'd been aiming for the number three next to it.

She'd been too embarrassed to confess to Pete. And then she'd been too alarmed. Pete had stared at her coldly, as if she'd slapped him in the face. That reaction had caused her to miss the next shot.

Chad and Megan had continued their kissing game, but Pete, when his turn came around, had glared at her before picking up his cue stick and running the table.

The game was over. Both games.

She'd gone to bed immediately.

With a sigh, she shoved back the covers and swung her legs to the floor. Her big toe stubbed the book she'd been reading. Dick Francis's latest mystery was on the floor beside the bed. She was going to have to stock her library if she was going to bed at eight o'clock each evening.

The door opened and she grabbed the blankets, clutching them to her chest like some virgin fearing ravishment. Pete stared at her from across the room.

"I didn't expect you to be awake," he said in a voice she couldn't read. "Are you okay?"

"I'm fine."

"Are you getting up?"

"In a few minutes. I was waiting for you to finish in the bathroom."

"If you want hot water, you'd better get in there before Brett." A smile broke out on his face. "He's notorious for long ones that leave the rest of us yelping when the hot water disappears. Jake makes him wait half an hour until the rest of us have finished." His grin was relaxed, letting Janie breathe easier.

"Thanks for warning me."

Pete looked at his watch. "You've still got five minutes."

Janie wondered if he expected her to parade past him into the bathroom. Not that her pajamas were

X-rated. On the contrary, they were cotton flannel. Definitely unsexy. Even so, she didn't intend to build any intimacy between them.

"Shall I tell Red you'll be down for breakfast?"

Would a message to Red convince him to go away? "Yes, please, but I probably won't make it down until after you're gone."

Pete stiffened, as if she'd insulted him. Then he began walking toward her. "In that case, I reckon I'll collect my goodbye kiss now."

Janie stared at him, her mouth falling open. The man was insane. "But, Pete, we don't have an audience. There's no reason to—"

Before she could finish her protest, he'd lifted her up from the bed, holding her against his chest, his mouth stopping her words.

Bacon in a hot frying pan didn't sizzle as much as her body did at Pete's touch. His hands slid up her back, caressing her skin, warming it. When one hand moved to her breast, her mind shut down and the heat intensified.

Then she was sliding down his strong body, landing with a thump on her bed.

Pete drew in a deep breath and marched across the room. "See if you can make a pool shot after *that* kiss."

Then he disappeared from sight.

TRUE TO HER PREDICTION, Janie didn't make it to the kitchen until the men had left. She made sure of it.

As she was eating the breakfast Red insisted on preparing, she asked, "Red, are you going into town today?"

"I'm not sure. Why? Is there something you need?"

"I thought I'd catch a ride over to my parents'. There are a few things I forgot to pack, and I'd like to get my car."

"You can take one of the pickups," Red offered.

"But then I couldn't drive my car back."

Megan entered the kitchen.

"I know. Maybe I can talk Megan into helping me," Janie suggested, smiling at her sister-in-law. She explained her need, and Megan quickly agreed to drive her.

"I don't know," Red said, scratching his head. "I'm not sure the boys would want you running around like that. You might get stuck or something."

Megan laughed and crossed the room to kiss Red's cheek. "Dear Red. There's nothing you can do to stop us. I have my own car, remember? And we're their wives, not their personal slaves."

Red backed off. "Okay, okay."

"In fact," Megan said, excitement rising in her voice, "why don't we call B.J. and see if she can meet us in town for lunch?"

Janie was amazed at the excitement that filled her. She hadn't realized how trapped she'd been feeling. "That's a great idea."

"Here now, you two don't like my cooking?"

"Don't be silly, Red. We just need a day out. Janie, we can leave early and shop for the babies' room. Then, when you and Pete go shopping, you'll know where to direct him so he'll choose what you like."

Megan's enthusiasm spurred Janie on. After Megan called B.J. and made arrangements for lunch, they began making a list of what they intended to do with their day.

"What am I supposed to tell the boys when they come in for lunch?" Red asked a bit nervously.

"Sit down and eat?" Janie suggested, and giggled.

Red smiled back. "You know those two lovelorn coyotes will be lookin' for you."

"Tell them we've gone to spend their hard-earned money, so eat fast and go earn some more," Megan told him. "Now, I'm going to do an hour or two of work before we need to leave."

"Shall I help you with the dishes, Red?" Janie offered.

"Nope. Won't take a minute to clean up after you two."

"Well, then, I'm starting some laundry. I'll do a load of bath towels first." With a sense of purpose in her step, Janie headed upstairs to gather the morning's trail of laundry left by four handsome cowboys.

PETE WONDERED how Janie would greet him. His parting words had shown his irritation with the events of the previous night. He regretted revealing his vulnerability to her.

"You comin', Pete?" Jake called from the barn door.

"Yeah, I'll be right there. Lester has something caught in his shoe." He bent over to pick up his mount's hoof.

"Need any help?"

"Naw. I'm coming." What was he doing, anyway? Hiding from some female? Even if she was his wife, no woman was going to cause Pete Randall to turn tail and run.

"Where are Brett and Chad?" he asked Jake as he joined him.

"They've already headed to the house. I was surprised you weren't with them. You and Chad seem to have females on the brain lately," Jake teased.

"Yeah." She was still on his brain. But he was reluctant to face her. He didn't want her to know how much he wanted her.

Jake gave him a strange look, but they'd reached the porch. When the two men entered the house, Pete's gaze scanned the room, searching for the woman he'd just assured himself he didn't want to see.

Chad was slumped down at the table.

"What's wrong?" Pete demanded.

"Nothing. The girls went shopping," Chad said, shifting his chin to his raised hand.

Pete stared at him, stunned. "Shopping? What for? What did Janie need?"

"Didn't need nothin'," Red assured him as he handled a pan of biscuits. "They're just bein' female."

"Careful, Red. That sounds like a sexist remark," Jake said.

"Jake!" Brett exclaimed. "First you're reading about pregnant women, and now you're talking about sexist remarks? What's going on around here?"

Jake looked uncomfortable, but he muttered, "We have to be more sensitive to—to things if we're going to have women around. I don't want any more divorces in the Randall family."

Pete wondered if Janie's nausea from her pregnancy felt anything like his stomach right this moment. The thought of divorce, of Janie leaving him, was more than he could bear.

But that had been his problem all along, hadn't it?

The question stunned him. Was that why he'd never sought marriage or any permanent relationship? He feared he might not survive its ending?

He hurriedly dismissed such wayward thoughts. He needed to think about Janie's actions today. "What do you think, Chad?"

Chad looked up at him in surprise. "Megan's not leaving me. There won't be any divorce from my marriage."

"No! No, I didn't mean that. I mean about today. What should we do about today?"

Chad still looked surprised. "What do you mean?"

Pete was beginning to question his own sanity. Why was Chad so confused? "I mean about them going off to town."

Jake cleared his throat. "There's no reason they shouldn't go to town, Pete. We're not holding them prisoners here."

"No, of course not. I just thought maybe they might get stuck on the road, or have a flat tire, or..." Pete didn't finish his sentence, because he couldn't think of any other disasters. He didn't like realizing he was being ridiculous.

"I do need someone to go into town and pick up the part for the snowplow before we have a new storm," Jake said, watching Pete. "You want to take care of that this afternoon?"

"I can do it," Brett said. "I've got an order of office supplies I need to pick up. And there are a couple of things I forgot."

Jake frowned at him.

"What?" Brett asked, bewilderment on his face.

"Pete needs to go into town, not you."

"But I really do need to add to my list."

"Give it to Pete. He'll take care of it for you," Jake insisted.

Brett snorted in derision. "Pete's computer illiterate. He'd get the wrong stuff."

"It's okay, Jake," Pete began, realizing how hard his older brother was working to provide him with an excuse to check on Janie.

"Maybe you should both go," Jake said, ignoring Pete's words. "That way neither one of you will do anything crazy."

"Hey!" Brett protested.

Pete didn't say anything. He was feeling a little crazy today. With Brett along, he'd have to pretend everything was normal.

"That okay with you, Chad?" Jake asked. "I really can't spare you if these other two go off."

"Sure. I know Megan will be back this afternoon."

Pete wished he had as much confidence. Somehow he feared Janie might have decided she'd made a mistake. But he was determined to prove her wrong.

THERE WEREN'T too many choices for lunch in Rawhide. B.J. had agreed to meet them at Marietta's Sandwich Shop, opened recently by a friend of Janie's mother.

Janie relaxed as she, B.J. and Megan chatted about fashions, food and gossip. B.J. was just getting to know her way around and had a lot of questions about her customers. Megan, too, wanted to know about some of the people she'd met. Having lived in the area all her life, Janie was supplying the information, among other things, while they ate their sandwiches.

"I love Red's cooking," Megan said, "but it's nice to eat something a little lighter occasionally. Living on the ranch, I'm afraid I'm gonna look like a cow!"

Janie laughed. "I know what you mean. But it takes a lot of calories to keep a cowboy in the saddle all day."

"Do you miss the work?" B.J. asked.

"Yes, but I guess I don't have a choice until after the babies are born."

"And after they're born, you won't have any time or energy for ranching," B.J. added.

"Really? I don't mean to sound naive, but I've never been around babies all that much."

"Me, neither," Megan added.

B.J. grinned. "I found one a challenge. I can't imagine dealing with two babies at once. I think part of the problem is that you don't get any uninterrupted sleep so you can regain your health."

"I'll be there to help you, though, Janie," Megan hurriedly assured her. "In fact, I'm planning on using your babies as a training experience. Chad is—is interested in having a family." Her cheeks pinkened, and she looked down at her sandwich.

"I guess we can learn together," Janie agreed, but her heart was envious of Megan's happiness. Pete hadn't had any choice about having a family, and Janie wasn't sure he would've chosen that option if given a chance.

Several acquaintances dropped by to chat with them, and Janie made sure her friends met them all. She was discovering the luxury of having friends nearby, and she wanted to be sure B.J. and Megan settled in happily.

When a warm hand rested on her shoulder, she turned with a smile, expecting another neighbor. Instead, she discovered Bryan Manning.

"Oh, hello, Bryan. How are you?"

"Fine. How about you? Liking married life?"

His penetrating stare brought a flush to her cheeks. She looked down at her plate. "Yes, of course. Have you met B. J. Anderson, the new vet, and Megan Randall, my sister-in-law?"

He barely spared the others a greeting but immediately turned his attention back to Janie. "I was surprised by your wedding."

"Yes, well, it all happened very suddenly."

"You told me you weren't marrying him."

Janie felt irritation surge through her. She had owed Bryan an explanation, and she'd called him the day before her marriage. He had protested her plans, and he didn't sound any happier about them now. But it was her business.

"I also called and told you I'd changed my mind, Bryan. That's a woman's prerogative."

"That's anyone's prerogative," Megan chimed in, smiling at the man. "I know because I'm an interior designer and my customers always change their minds. Usually just after I've purchased some outlandish piece of furniture that only they would want."

Janie was grateful for Megan's lighthearted attempt. It had no effect on Bryan. He was undeterred.

"My offer still stands," he said insistently, putting his hand back on Janie's shoulder.

Her irritation worsened. Shrugging her shoulder so he would remove his hand, she said, "Thanks, but I've made my choice, Bryan. I'm not planning on changing my mind."

"Look, can I speak to you alone? We could move to another table for a few minutes, have a cup of coffee together...."

"No, Bryan. I'm sorry, but we have nothing to say to each other."

He seemed almost as irritated as Janie, but she felt no sympathy for him. He was a handsome man, but she wasn't sure what she'd seen in him. When she'd phoned him, he'd been difficult, but she'd thought

he'd understood. Now all he was doing was harass-
ing her.

"Janie, why don't we go pay our bill and meet you
at the door in a couple of minutes," Megan suggested.

"I'm not sure—"

"Thanks," Bryan said, nodding to Megan in grat-
itude.

As soon as the other two left the table, Bryan sat
down. "Janie, I know you felt you had to marry the
father of your baby, but I was willing to adopt the
baby, to let it be mine."

"Yes, and I appreciate that, Bryan, but I made my
choice, and I don't intend to change my mind." Ap-
parently he hadn't heard there would be two babies.
But she thought she'd made the right decision even if
there were only one baby. She now believed that Pete
should have a role in his children's lives.

If only he wanted to have a part in her life, too.

"Can I at least call you, talk to you occasionally?
I can't just walk away from you."

Janie almost gasped as she envisioned Pete's reaction to a call from Bryan, his chief competition. "I
don't think that would be a good idea, Bryan. You
need to get on with your life."

"But I love you!"

They were the words she wanted to hear from Pete.
Not from Bryan. "I'm sorry, Bryan, but any relationship we had is over. I'm married."

His hand reached out to cover hers as it lay on the
table. Why couldn't the man understand what she was

telling him? She tugged at his hold on her, but he didn't let go.

"Bryan—" she began, but an icy voice interrupted her.

"Take your hand off my wife."

She didn't need to turn around to know that Pete had arrived on the scene and that he was angry.

"Pete, I'll take care of this."

"You're my wife. I'll take care of it." Pete reached over her shoulder and grasped Bryan's wrist. "Turn her loose."

"You're acting like a caveman," Bryan protested even as he did as Pete asked. "In Chicago, we're a little more civilized."

"I'm sure. And if you want to live a long and fruitful life, I'd suggest you hightail it right back to Chicago. Hitting on another man's wife out here will get you a broken nose."

"Pete!" Janie protested. The last thing she wanted was a scene in front of half the town two days after her marriage.

"Listen here, cowboy, you're not going to tell me what to do!" Bryan unwisely responded.

"The hell I won't!" Pete said. He punctuated his words with a blow to the man's nose.

Bryan crumpled to the floor, and everyone stared at Janie and Pete.

Chapter Thirteen

Brett, Megan and B.J. rushed to the table, arriving about the same time Bryan hit the floor.

"Pete! What are you doing?" Brett demanded, grabbing his brother by the arm.

"Protecting my wife," Pete growled.

Janie closed her eyes briefly and then glared at her husband. "I wasn't in any danger."

B.J. helped Bryan to his feet. She felt his nose even as she offered him a napkin to staunch the flow of blood. "I don't think anything is broken, Mr. Manning. But I'm sure Pete will be glad to pay the doctor bill if you want to go see Dr. Jacoby."

Brett quickly seconded B.J.'s offer, but Pete didn't. Janie could still see anger in his eyes as he looked at Bryan. She tugged on her husband's arm. "Pete, let's get out of here."

Without a word, he took her hand and led her outside. Once they were apart from the others, he turned on her. "What were you doing with that man?" The anger dripped from his voice.

"Trying to avoid causing a scene," she replied in kind. "Wasted effort, as it turns out, since you decided to play Tarzan."

"You *wanted* to talk to him?"

"No, Pete, I don't ever want to talk to him again. He was being insistent, which I didn't like, but I didn't think I was in any danger."

Pete looked away, staring across the almost empty street. He removed his hat and ran a hand through his hair. "Probably you weren't," he said on an exhaled breath. He kept looking away as he continued, "But if I'm Tarzan, you are *my* Janie, and I won't have that man hanging around you."

Janie didn't know what to make of this man. He both infuriated her and turned her on—all at the same time. Then something occurred to her. "What are you doing in town?"

The guilty look on his face confirmed her suspicions. But he hurriedly said, "Jake wanted me to pick up a part for the snowplow."

"You were here to check on me, weren't you?" she demanded. "Do you think I can't be trusted out of your sight? Do you intend to follow me all over creation?"

"Now, honey—"

"Did I need a note from you to have lunch in town?" She was shouting at him now, unmindful of the people in the parking lot. "Are you afraid I'll spend all your money? Damn it, Pete! I don't even know if you have money. You won't let me do anything. You just want to keep me wrapped in cotton and sitting in a corner somewhere!" She feared she might've gone too far, but it felt good to release some of her frustration.

"Janie, are you all right?" Megan asked behind her, putting a hand on her arm.

Janie turned to see Brett, Megan and B.J. watching her, and she promptly burst into tears.

PETE SWEPT JANIE up into his arms and carried her to his pickup. B.J. followed and opened the door to the cab, then closed it behind Janie.

"Pete, emotional swings are normal with pregnancy. Humor her, okay?"

"Don't you think I should take her to Doc?" he asked, surprised.

"Nope. Everything's fine. She probably got a little tired today. Let her take a nap, and pretend this crying jag never happened."

"But it's so unlike Janie."

"It's unlike a nonpregnant Janie. Things are different now."

You could say that again.

Megan and Brett joined them.

"Are you taking Janie home?" Brett asked.

"Yeah. She needs a nap."

"But she wanted her car from her parents' house," Megan explained.

"So she can run around and get exhausted again?" Pete demanded.

"So she won't feel trapped," Megan said quietly. "Pregnancy is new to Janie at the moment, Pete. Letting her have her car won't hurt anything."

"And it's not as if you have a choice," B.J. argued. "She's an adult. Adults get to make their own decisions."

He stared at Janie, sitting in the cab of his truck, wiping the tears from her eyes. She looked at him and then hurriedly turned away. *She hates me.* The thought struck him with such force, he almost reeled back. What was he going to do? Hate was definitely not the emotion he wanted from her.

"Fine. We'll go by her parents and let her pick up her car. But I'm getting her a cellular phone so she can call if she gets in trouble."

"Good idea. You take her on back home, and I'll arrange for the cellular phone," Brett said. "That is, I will if you can spare the time, Megan, 'cause I don't have my truck here with me."

"Of course I can. Why are you both in town, anyway? I thought you were shorthanded at the ranch."

Pete's cheeks turned red, but he confessed, "Jake thought up an excuse 'cause I was worried about Janie. I knew she wouldn't want me to check on her, but—but I was imagining all kinds of disasters."

"You mean like someone punching another person out and causing a scene?" B.J. teased.

Pete reluctantly grinned. "Something like that."

After telling them all goodbye, he circled the truck and got in. Janie stared straight ahead.

"Honey, I'll run you by your folks' so you can pick up your car. I didn't think about you needing it."

She turned to stare at him, surprise on her face.

Finally he'd done something right, thanks to Megan and B.J. Maybe he'd take his marriage problems to those two instead of his brothers. Women seemed to understand other women better than any man did.

JANIE TOOK A LONG NAP, something she never used to do. But she'd learned that everything had changed since she'd become pregnant. And married.

When she came down to dinner, Pete was waiting for her, a wary look on his face. She couldn't blame him. Her crying had been almost as awkward and bizarre as his scene with Bryan.

But she didn't want to talk about the afternoon's events. It brought her emotions too close to the surface. She had to keep her distance from the sexy man she'd married.

Which was hard to do when he took the seat next to her, his broad shoulders touching hers every time he passed a dish to her. It simply wasn't fair, she decided. Why did he have to be so attractive?

After dinner, she insisted on helping Red clean up. It would give her some distance from Pete. But when Megan volunteered, too, Pete assured her he would help Janie in a voice that brooked no argument.

"You really don't have to," she protested anyway. So much for distance!

"You let him be, Janie. He needs to do his share. After all, he didn't work this afternoon," Red added, chuckling. "Unless you call rounding up one little stray hard work."

"I hadn't strayed, Red. I was with Megan and B.J."

"And was it Megan and B.J. this old grizzly bear punched out?" Red was more amused by his own humor than his audience was.

"That's enough, Red," Pete warned sternly. "This afternoon is best forgotten."

"Good idea," Brett agreed, "but it won't happen around town very soon. Everyone was talking about it."

Janie groaned. She'd never want to venture into town again.

"I think it's sweet that he's so jealous just because another man wanted to talk to you," Megan said.

"I'd be just as jealous, Meggie," Chad assured her with a growl.

"Good." Megan patted his cheek, and he leaned over to kiss her temple.

Janie turned away with a stack of dishes. Megan was right. She should appreciate Pete's...interest. But she would've traded that possessiveness in a minute for just one caress given with love.

Pete arrived at the sink beside her. "Sure you're up to this? I can handle the dishes if you're too tired."

"No, thank you. I had a long nap today."

Polite. They were being exceptionally polite around each other tonight, as if they were strangers.

"Okay. I'll wash and you dry."

He handed her a dish towel, and Janie took a step back. When she got too close to him, she had to fight a ridiculous urge to throw herself at him.

Distracted, she began running water in the sink.

"I'll wash," Pete repeated. "There's no point in you getting dishpan hands." Without warning, he put his hands on her waist and shifted her over.

The warmth of his touch was wonderful but all too brief. She really was going to have to get her hormones under control.

They completed the dishes with only occasional words exchanged, all surface, all polite.

Pete invited her to come watch a special on television afterward, but she refused. She couldn't take more close contact with him without losing control completely.

Going upstairs, she ran some hot water in the tub and added bath bubbles. After the difficult day she'd had, she needed some soothing.

She would've preferred Pete's hands to do that job, but she couldn't ask him. He was treating her like a stranger, someone he didn't know. Not like his lover.

Of course, she wasn't.

But she wanted to be again.

By the time the water had cooled, she was sleepy. Changing into her pajamas, she slipped under the covers, ready to go to sleep.

A knock on the bathroom door did away with all that relaxation. "Yes?"

"It's Pete. May I come in?"

"Of course." She pulled the covers to her chin.

"You're really going to sleep?"

"Why, yes."

"Oh. I bought you something today while I was in town."

"I know. Megan told me. The cellular phone. I appreciate it, Pete, but I don't think I need it tonight."

"No. I mean, yes, I bought you the phone, but I bought you something else, too."

Curiosity filled her. "What?"

"I noticed you were reading Dick Francis. When we were in the bookstore today, I saw his latest in hardback and I bought it for you." He pulled his hand from behind his back and held out the book to her.

Janie's eyes filled. Drat the tears! She never cried, but right now she was so moved by his kindness. "Thank you, Pete. I'll enjoy reading it. That was very thoughtful of you."

He brought the book over to her. "I'll leave it here by your bed. I didn't realize I'd need it, but I guess it's kind of an apology for, you know, hitting Bryan."

"It's all right. He probably deserved it."

Pete seemed surprised by her words, but she'd long forgiven his actions this afternoon.

"Thanks. Then—then I guess I'll say good-night."

He bent down and kissed her brow. Janie, expecting a real kiss, like this morning's, found herself empty and unfulfilled as he left her room, closing the door behind him.

Now he was really being too polite.

But she couldn't blame him. The fault was her own. He was only complying with her request. His promise to renegotiate their agreement after the babies were born had made her believe he still wanted her. Now she wasn't so sure.

Had her refusal to let their marriage be a real one killed even his desire for her?

He was such a special man. His thoughtfulness proved that. And no matter how staunchly she tried to deny it, she loved him. In fact, she always had.

What was she going to do now? Seduce him? Tell him she'd changed her mind? Send out an invitation to her bed? Move back into his bed?

She fell asleep debating her alternatives.

THE REST OF THE FAMILY sat in the television room, watching a special. During advertisements, Megan told Chad about the baby cribs she and Janie had found that morning.

"They're the only matched pair in town, so it was nice that Janie liked them. I hope she and Pete buy them before one is sold."

Jake, sitting nearby, leaned forward. "Did you see them?"

"Oh, yes, we studied them for half an hour. Janie fell in love with them, and I did, too. She said when— I mean, if—Chad and I have a baby, we'd be able to use them, too."

Jake grinned. "That's right. Start a family tradition with special baby cribs. Where are they?"

"McAnally's. We looked at sheets and bumper pads, but the ones Janie liked have to be ordered."

"Did she place an order?" Jake asked.

"Well, no, she wanted to wait until Pete had a chance to look at them," Megan explained.

"Would you have time to go into town tomorrow afternoon with me? I'd like to buy that stuff as a surprise for them," Jake said. Looking at his two younger brothers and Red, he added, "A surprise. Got that, guys?"

With big grins, the others nodded their compliance.

THE NEXT MORNING, after breakfast, Janie called her mother. During their conversation, Janie realized what she needed to do. She would return to her parents' each morning and do half a day's work on her father's computer, keeping his paperwork up-to-date.

At least until the babies were born. Or until she got too big to get behind the steering wheel of her car.

Excitement filled her at the promise of having some direction to her days. She put in a load of laundry, as she had yesterday, and returned to their rooms to tidy up.

And, as she'd decided last night, there was one other chore she had to do.

When she left the house an hour later, she warned Red she wouldn't be there for lunch.

"Again? Does that mean Pete will lose another afternoon of work?" Red asked.

"No. I'll be eating at home with my mom and dad. Pete knows I'll be okay there. Then I'll come back here after lunch and take my nap. I'm a lady of leisure, you know," she added, grinning.

"Yeah. Right," Red snorted in derision. "That's why you've already started the laundry, isn't it?"

"Just trying to be helpful," Janie said with a smile, and kissed his cheek. "See you later."

PETE MISSED JANIE at lunch. But, as she had fore-seen, he couldn't complain about her visiting her family. At least Red assured him she'd taken the cel-lular phone with her.

After eating, he paused to call the Dawsons. Lavi-nia answered the phone.

"Lavinia, it's Pete. Is Janie there?"

"Yes, she is, Pete. Just a moment."

"I'm not checking on you," he said immediately when Janie came to the phone. "I just wanted to be sure you were feeling all right."

"I'm fine, Pete."

"Well, I didn't see you this morning," he said, lowering his voice, hoping his family wouldn't hear. "So I thought..."

"Everything's fine except that I'm expanding at a rapid rate. I had a hard time fastening my jeans this morning. You'll think I'm fat."

Pete didn't need any advice on how to respond to her complaint. From his heart, he said, "No, I'll think you're beautiful, just like I do now."

When only silence was her answer, he thought he'd upset her again.

Then very quietly she said, "Thank you, Pete."

"Janie? You're not crying, are you?"

"No. But we need to t-talk."

His heart contracted with fear. Had she changed her mind about being married to him? Was she going to stay at her parents' house? "Do you want me to come over now?" he asked gruffly, trying to hide the panic he was feeling.

"No! No, I'll be home in a little while. We can talk this evening. It's nothing urgent."

Nothing urgent. What did that mean? After telling her goodbye, he hung up the phone and stood there, staring into space.

"Pete?" Jake called to him.

"Yeah?"

"I'm going into town for a while. Take charge, okay?"

"Sure. Is there anything I can do for you? Why do you need to go into town today?"

He was surprised when Jake avoided his gaze.

"Just something I need to take care of."

The last time Jake had acted so suspicious, he'd been trying to find wives for them all. "You going into town to find a wife for Brett?" Pete teased, hoping to lighten his own spirits.

"Hey!" Brett protested. "I'm happy being single. At least I don't have to go around punching anybody's lights out."

"Your time will come, little brother," Jake warned him with a grin, but he didn't give Pete any further explanation for his trip to town.

When Pete got back to the house about dark, he was tired, but he was pretty sure his lack of energy stemmed from the mental exercises he wrestled with all afternoon. What did Janie want to talk about?

When he opened the back door, he was relieved to see her in the kitchen. If nothing else, she'd come back this time.

With a sigh, he crossed the room and wrapped his arms around her. He couldn't risk a kiss that might destroy what little control he had, so he gave her a peck on the cheek.

"Hi. How was your visit with your parents?"

"Fine," she returned, but Pete noticed she didn't look at him as she stepped from his embrace. "I'm going to go over every morning and do some paperwork for my dad. He's going to continue to pay me a salary, too."

"You don't need a salary!" Pete protested. "I'm getting you a checkbook for my account."

"I like to feel that I'm contributing, and no one will let me do anything around here."

"You're doing laundry," Red called out from the pantry, "and helping out in the kitchen."

"And I appreciate your letting me help, Red. It makes me feel a part of—of the family," Janie said, smiling at Pete.

Like a flash of lightning in a summer storm, Janie's words suddenly illuminated a problem, and Pete realized he'd made a big mistake. In his attempts to care for her, Pete had shut her out. Or at least it seemed that's how it appeared to her. Frowning, he scrambled for ways to involve Janie in his life.

"Are you good at the computer?"

Over her shoulder as she carried silverware to the table, she said coolly, "Very good. Why?"

"Reckon you could teach me?"

That question stopped her in her tracks. She spun around to stare at him. "Are you serious?"

He licked his dry lips, anxious for her response. "Yeah. Brett says I'm helpless, but I thought maybe you'd be a better teacher."

She smiled at him with real warmth, and he felt it all the way to his toes. Janie had to be the only woman who could turn him on talking about computers. But then, she could turn him on anywhere, anytime.

"I'd love to teach you. Do you have your own computer?"

"Nope. Just the one in the office Brett uses. But if you know what to buy, we can go get whatever we need."

Jake, having entered the kitchen in time to hear part of Pete's response, said, "What are we buying now? This family is turning into shopaholics."

Pete remembered that Jake had gone into town. "Was that what you were doing today?"

Jake smiled but didn't answer as the rest of the family trooped in. "What were you talking about buying?"

"A new computer," Pete said.

Brett, sitting down at the table, groaned. "Come on, Pete, you don't need a computer. You don't even know how to turn one on."

"Janie's going to teach me."

Brett turned to Janie. "You have no idea what a gargantuan task that's going to be."

"Pete will do just fine," Janie assured her brother-in-law and then smiled at Pete.

Pete vowed to stay up nights studying if it pleased Janie. If learning computers made her feel more a part of their family, then he'd learn computers. If computers kept her there, a part of his life, then he'd build one from scratch. Whatever it took.

"So where will you put the computer?" Jake asked, frowning. "Not in the babies' room."

"No, of course not," Janie said calmly. "If necessary, we can put it in our bedroom."

Pete liked the sound of that, *our bedroom*. He only wished it were true.

"There's a small room, not much bigger than a bathroom, just down the hall from your bedroom. We've been using it for storage, haven't we, Red?" Jake asked.

"Yep. Lots of stuff that needs to be thrown out."

"We'll convert it into an office for the two of you," Jake offered. "After all, with Pete's venture with the rodeos, I imagine you'll have a lot of records and files."

"Yeah. More than I can deal with," Pete agreed, thinking about the fat files of papers he had stacked in a corner in Jake's office.

"We'll take care of that, thanks, Jake," Janie said. Then she launched into a discussion of computers and computer programs with Brett with more animation than Pete had seen since their marriage.

He relaxed a little. Maybe they were going to make it after all. If he made Janie happy, she might agree to stay with him. Him and the babies.

After dinner, before anyone could leave the table, Jake cleared his throat. "Pete and Janie, I want to explain why I went to town today."

Janie looked puzzled, but Pete felt a sinking feeling in his stomach. What was going on?

"Megan said you found the cribs you wanted yesterday, Janie, and we bought them today for you. I was afraid if we waited, they might sell one of them.''

Janie's face lit up. ''Oh, thank you, Jake. That's so thoughtful of you. Pete, you don't mind, do you?''

''No, of course not. I should've— I didn't realize we'd need to buy that stuff so early.''

''We don't, but it will be fun to begin putting together our nursery,'' she assured him, beaming.

Whatever made her happy.

''Great. So, let's all go to the Randall nursery and put these suckers together,'' Jake ordered, and rose from the table, followed by the rest of the family.

They were going to the nursery! His family was going to the nursery that was Janie's bedroom. They were about to discover the truth about his marriage.

Pete stared at Janie, panic filling him.

She smiled back serenely.

Chapter Fourteen

"No!" Pete said, jumping to his feet.

"Why not?" Jake asked, pausing on his way to the door, the rest of the family following.

"Uh, you must have lots to do. There's no rush. I can put them together some other time."

"But I'd love to see them put together tonight, Pete, if you don't mind," Janie said, moving over to touch his arm.

Damn. He'd promised himself he'd do whatever made her happy. He shrugged his shoulders and muttered, "Okay." He was about to be humiliated before his brothers. He only hoped Janie appreciated the sacrifice.

He received a small reward. Janie leaned against him and lightly brushed her lips against his, then took his hand and led him up the stairs behind the others.

The sweetness of her gestures almost made him forget what was about to happen. Almost. But he'd have difficulty facing his brothers once they discovered that his wife wouldn't even share the same room with him. He thought about heading out to the barn instead of their rooms, but he couldn't do that to Janie.

"Uh, the rooms may be a little messy. Janie—"

"I straightened everything this afternoon," she promised, interrupting him. "Our bedroom isn't too messy."

Our bedroom. There was that phrase again. And she squeezed his hand.

"We don't even need to go in there," Jake assured him. "Just the babies' room. And since they haven't arrived yet, it shouldn't be too big a mess."

Pete weakly returned his brother's grin.

"I hope you like the cribs, Pete," Janie said beside him. "They're all white, but I thought we'd put sheets and bumper pads with a circus theme. And we could get that lady who lives near Rawhide to come out and do a mural on the wall."

"That would be so cute, wouldn't it, Pete?" Megan said.

"Yeah, cute." If Janie wanted a mural, he'd agree to every wall in the house being painted. But right now his insides were quivering as Jake opened the door to the nursery.

Several big boxes rested against one wall.

"We brought these up earlier while Janie was taking a nap," Jake explained, crossing the room.

Pete was several steps into the room, his eyes searching for anything that would betray their secret, when he realized what Jake had said. While Janie was taking her nap. Why hadn't Jake seen her on the daybed? He turned to look at Janie.

"You must've been quiet as can be...or I was sleeping like a log, because I never heard a thing."

Feeling befuddled, it took Pete a minute to realize that Janie must've been sleeping in the bedroom. *Our bedroom.* He stared at her. Why? Did she always take her naps in there while he was at work? He'd gotten the impression she was never going to darken the door to that room again.

She smiled at him as if nothing of significance had happened and crossed the room to watch his brothers start taking the cribs from the boxes.

"I figure if we divide up into two teams, we'll have these put together in no time," Jake said.

The men quickly turned their activity into a competition with bets on who would finish first. Janie, Megan and Red became the cheering sections.

"I only hope they don't leave something out just to get finished faster," Megan said loudly enough for everyone to hear.

"They won't," Janie replied confidently. "Pete wouldn't let them. He wants everything perfect for the babies."

Pete wanted to tell her how right she was. And the most perfect thing for his babies would be for their mother to want to stay there with him. To love him.

He heaved a sigh. He'd finally admitted it. He needed Janie to love him. And he needed to love her.

"You okay?" Brett asked, working alongside him.

"Yeah. It makes the babies seem more real to be putting these things together."

"It does, doesn't it?" Jake agreed. "Next year we'll be putting together trains and tricycles and stuff for

Christmas." The spark lighting his eyes made everyone laugh.

"You mean dollhouses, don't you, Jake?" Janie teased.

"Okay, but only if they're girls. I'm not putting together dollhouses for my nephews."

"Maybe we'll have one of each," Janie said, wrapping her arms over her stomach.

Pete's mouth went dry, and he wanted to hold her against him, to feel the growth of his children in her, to love her.

Janie had been right about his being afraid any woman he loved would leave him. Whether it was his mother's death, several past romances or Chloe's leaving Jake, he'd been afraid.

But Janie had gotten under his defenses. He'd fallen in love with her without realizing it. When she'd broken off with him, he'd felt he was dying. But he hadn't admitted his love.

Then, with the babies, he'd gotten a second chance. This time he wasn't going to blow it. He wouldn't overwhelm her. He'd take it slow and easy, and keep her happy. And quite possibly die of sexual frustration. But that was a small sacrifice to keep Janie in his life.

"Come on, Pete. We don't have time for daydreaming," Brett warned, poking him in the ribs.

He took his gaze off Janie and returned it to the task at hand. In no time, both cribs were ready.

Janie walked over and smoothed her hand across the small mattresses, first one and then the other. Then she turned to Pete. "Do you like them?"

Pete would've claimed to like the ugliest cribs in creation to please Janie. But he did like these.

"Yeah, I do. They look great."

She turned to look at them again, beaming, and leaned back against him.

Pete couldn't help it. His arms came around to cradle her against him. He was in heaven.

"Thanks, guys," Janie said, her voice sounding a little weepy. "What a wonderful surprise."

Pete tightened his hold on her, loving the feel of her against him, wanting to comfort her.

"Our pleasure, Janie," Jake replied. "We want you to know how happy we are you married Pete and how excited we are about the babies."

The others nodded.

"And we hope to use these beds next," Chad added.

"Chad!" Megan protested.

"Well, we do. We're just not sure when." Chad winked at his brothers. "We're working on it really hard, though."

"Chad Randall!" Megan protested again, more vehemently.

Everyone laughed, but Jake suggested they get out of Pete and Janie's rooms and let them have some time to themselves.

The family filed out, but much to Pete's delight, Janie didn't move, staying wrapped in his arms. He leaned his head against her silky hair, loving the fresh smell of it.

"Chad's funny, but I'm not sure Megan was amused," Janie said.

"I don't think she really minded."

"No, probably not."

Unimportant dialogue, he knew. What was important was being said by their bodies. Pete only hoped Janie wasn't put off by the response he couldn't hold back.

"Pete."

"Hmm," he replied casually, rubbing his face against her hair, concentrating on the feel of her, the scent of her.

"Remember when I said we needed to talk?"

He felt as if someone had doused him with a bucket of cold water. "Yeah. You want to talk now?"

She tensed against him, and he let his arms fall as he took a step backward.

"I think we should," she said as she turned to face him. But her gaze didn't rest on his face. She quickly looked away.

When she didn't say anything else, Pete thought he would die from the suspense. "Tell me, Janie," he ordered roughly, taking another step back.

"I— This is difficult for me to say."

His heart contracted as he prepared for the worst. She had decided to leave him. Why hadn't she told him before they'd put up the cribs? Why had she let him picture the two of them bending over the beds, watching their babies sleep, him holding Janie in his arms, as he had a moment earlier?

Closing his eyes, hoping to hide his pain, he waited for her to continue.

"I moved my things back into our bedroom."

Our bedroom. Pete's eyes shot open, and he stared at her. "What are you saying?" he demanded hoarsely.

She turned her back to him and walked to one of the cribs, running her fingertips over the smooth metal. "I want us to be really married." After a brief pause, she added, "If you want to."

He turned to stone. Having prepared himself for the worst, he found it impossible to speak or move.

"If you don't, it's okay. I can move my things back—" Janie began hurriedly, her head down.

"No!" Finally he came out of his trance and grabbed her by the shoulder, spinning her around. "Are you saying you want to sleep with me?" He didn't want to make any mistakes.

She nodded. "If you're not put off by my being fat and—"

Pete didn't waste words. He swooped down on her and lifted her against him, his lips covering hers in a heart-stopping, life-giving kiss. Her arms went around his neck, and she clung to him with an eagerness that fed his heart.

"Will we hurt the babies?" he asked, thinking he'd die if she said yes.

"No. Doc said there wouldn't be a problem about that for at least a few months."

With a heartfelt prayer of thanks, Pete carried her into the room he would forever call *our bedroom* now. He laid her down on the bed and began unbuttoning her shirt. "I want to see our babies growing in you, Janie. I want to touch every inch of you. I've missed you so much."

"Me, too," she whispered, her hands going to his shirt.

He unbuttoned her jeans and slid them down to reveal her stomach, reverently stroking her skin, feeling the slight mound his children had caused. Then he bent down to caress her stomach with his lips, each kiss a promise to love and protect his little family.

"Pete," Janie urged.

"Hmm?"

"I'm dying for you to kiss me. Please."

She didn't have to ask twice. Pete slid onto the bed beside her, and his lips joined with hers. His hands began the pleasant task of removing her clothes...and touching her to his heart's content.

"Your jeans," she finally whispered when his lips strayed once more, caressing first her neck, then her breasts.

He was willing to follow her urging. But he didn't want to stop what he was doing. She tasted so good...and he was so hungry for her. He stripped as quickly as possible and returned to her side. He was ready for her, and it appeared she was ready for him as she guided him to her.

Though he intended to go slowly and gently into her, he found his needs raging. Janie joined him, tempting him, caressing him, as she had the first time, and Pete couldn't hold back.

When they collapsed against each other, their breaths rasping, their hearts pounding, Pete wrapped his arms around her and held her against him. He never wanted her to leave.

JANIE LAY in Pete's arms, grateful for the decision she'd made. Grateful that he still wanted her. Grateful that she was here with him instead of in her single bed in the next room.

Last night she'd debated what she should do. She loved the big lug, but she'd tried to hold out for his love. Finally, she admitted to herself that he might never come to love her. But if there was a chance that he would, it would happen because she made him happy.

And she wasn't making him happy sleeping in the other room.

It didn't hurt that his loving satisfied the hunger in her for his touch. After six months of feeling him move inside her, of loving him with all her heart, she'd felt half alive apart from him.

So she was back in her lover's arms. Now all she had to do was convince him he loved her, as well as his babies.

She kissed his chest and snuggled closer. Combat duty had never been so comfy.

THE NEXT FEW DAYS whizzed by, filled with their loving and Janie's work at her parents' ranch. Pete was all consideration, helping her with anything she did when he was home.

When the two of them did the dishes the next night also, Jake decided to arrange a dish rotation. Chad and Megan, Pete and Janie, and Brett and Jake.

"Hey, I don't get female companionship," Brett complained. "I don't think I should have to do dishes."

"We have to train you so some woman will take you on," Jake assured him. "Women today expect a man to pitch in. Right, Janie, Megan?"

"Definitely," Janie answered.

"Of course," Megan agreed. "Are you in training, too, Jake?"

Pete, sitting next to Janie with his arm around her, saw Jake tense. Megan was a favorite with Jake, but her teasing had gone awry.

"No," he replied gruffly. "I've already tried."

"Don't you want children of your own, Jake?" Janie asked softly.

Pete's heart ached for his brother. The babies he and Janie were having meant everything to him. Well, almost everything. Janie meant the most. But Jake wasn't going to have anything.

"You're having two. I figured you'd share with me, Janie. How about that?" Jake tried to muster a smile, but he was still uptight.

"Okay. But I think you'd make some wonderful babies."

"Yeah, and you read that book," Brett added, a big grin on his face. "You ought to put all that knowledge to good use."

"What book?" Janie asked, pretending Megan hadn't already told her about it.

After glaring at his brother, Jake said, "A book about having babies. I wanted to be sure we were doing everything we needed to for you."

"That's so sweet of you, Jake," Janie said.

"Pete's reading it now."

Janie looked from Jake to Pete, smiling at him, and Pete wanted to make love to her at once. Which wasn't surprising since he wanted to make love to her morning, noon and night.

"Ready to go up?" he whispered in Janie's ear.

Her nod made his heart swell. He'd tried not to make too many demands on her, but she never said no.

"We're going to go on to bed now," he said, rising and pulling Janie after him.

"Now?" Brett asked in surprise. "But the movie's not over."

What Pete had in mind would be a lot more fun than any movie ever made. "Yeah, now."

"But—"

"Brett," Jake said softly, gaining his brother's attention.

"Yeah?" Brett answered, but he stared at Pete and Janie leaving the room.

Before Jake could speak, Megan and Chad said good-night and left the room.

"What's wrong with everyone?" Brett asked.

Jake sighed. Brett was twenty-nine. He hadn't thought he'd have to explain the birds and the bees again. "They're newlyweds, Brett. They're not interested in television."

"Yeah, but—but Pete and Janie have been together for a while. They're expecting already. Don't you—? I mean, I don't remember you and Chloe—" Brett broke off, as if suddenly aware that he might be stepping on his brother's toes.

"Nope, I don't, either. Which makes me hope these two marriages are a hell of a lot better than mine."

PETE WOKE JANIE UP with a kiss, not an unusual occurrence these days. "Hey, beautiful, want to go to town today?"

She ran her fingers through his chest hair, loving the feel of him. "Hmm, why?" Somehow she feared any change to their routine, as if it might make a difference in their marriage.

"It's Saturday. I thought we might go shopping for that computer you were talking about. I want to get started learning how to operate it. The paperwork is about to overtake me."

"Especially since you don't work on it in the evenings anymore."

"Yeah, you little seductress. You keep dragging me upstairs to seduce me."

"I believe," she said, putting a finger to his lips, "you carried me up the stairs last night. So who's seducing whom?"

"I only carried you up because I was trying to prove my manhood."

Pete's grin, so warm and inviting, had been in short supply the first few days of their marriage. It made Janie feel good to see him happy. "Um, I believe you have a better way to show your manhood than flexing your muscles, Pete."

"I don't know, sweetheart. I think I'm just making another muscle hard to please you." He nuzzled her neck.

"Well, it certainly is getting a workout," she whispered, reaching for him.

WHEN JANIE finally got down to the kitchen, after Pete had risen from their marriage bed late to work, she discovered B.J. at the table with Megan.

"Good morning. Good to see you, B.J."

"You too, Janie. You look a lot happier than you did at the boxing match in town."

"Shh," Megan said, a grin on her face. "We're not supposed to mention that, Pete's orders."

"Ah. Sorry, I didn't know the rules," B.J. returned with a grin.

"We're also not supposed to notice when Pete comes to breakfast very late," Megan added.

"Then I take it I shouldn't mention Chad's late arrival yesterday?" Janie said, her own grin in place.

Megan's cheeks flushed. With a chuckle, she said, "Probably not."

B.J. leaned back in her chair. "This place is a breeding ground for happy couples. Any sign of it spreading?"

"What do you mean?" Janie asked.

"I just wondered if Jake and Brett were showing any inclinations toward joining the happy throng."

"'Fraid not," Megan said with a sigh. "They're both staunch supporters of bachelorhood."

"Just as well," B.J. said with a shrug. "Their availability keeps half the women in the county hoping they'll look their way."

"True. And that's fine with me as long as they don't look at Pete," Janie said with a sigh.

"Or Chad," Megan added. And they grinned at each other.

PETE GOT BACK to the house a little after ten. He bounded up the stairs, anxious to see Janie. "Sweetheart, are you ready?" he asked as he opened the door.

She popped her head out of the bathroom, one bare shoulder enticing him forward.

"Almost. I just have to put on— Pete! What are you doing? You'll mess up my makeup," she warned him with a sexy chuckle as he pulled her against him.

"Okay, okay," he grumbled, moving back into the bedroom.

Janie stared at him, as if he'd grown two heads.

"What?" he asked, puzzled.

"Nothing." She turned back to the mirror.

He sat there drinking in her beauty, enjoying the slight hint of her pregnancy. It wasn't the same as making love to her, but it beat not being able to see her.

She came into the room and opened the closet door. The intimacy of watching her dress was new...and pleasurable. He hadn't had all that much experience with it. Usually he showered and left while she stayed in bed, recovering from their lovemaking.

"I'm ready," she said breathlessly, emerging from the closet as she slipped into a pair of pumps.

"You're kind of dressed up, aren't you?" he asked.

"I haven't gone too many places with my husband," she said. "I wanted to look nice for you."

He rose from the bed and took her in his arms. "Well, you sure succeeded, sweetheart." He kissed her until he realized he'd have to stop or take her to bed. She'd already nixed that plan.

So he'd take her to town to buy a computer. And show off his beautiful new wife. Whatever it took to make her happy.

And all the time, he'd be wishing they were back home, alone, making love.

Chapter Fifteen

He's already tired of me.

Janie watched her husband out of the corner of her eye as he drove the pickup to town. That had to be the answer to the puzzle. Before she'd gotten pregnant, Pete had never backed off making love to her.

Now all she had to say was stop, and he turned away.

She'd heard of married couples growing disinterested, but she'd never expected it to happen after one week.

"Something wrong?" Pete asked.

"No, why?"

"You were staring at me."

She smiled. "Just admiring your handsome mug," she said. "And wondering if our babies will look like you or me."

"You if they're girls. They'd be mighty upset if they looked like me."

"Would you be disappointed if they're girls?"

"You asked that before. All that matters is that they arrive safely, sweetheart. I'll be happy with either boys or girls. Or one of each." He reached out and took her hand in his, bringing it to rest on his strong thigh.

She shivered. Touching him made her want him all the more. She wanted to tell him she loved him. But that was a topic he didn't want to discuss. She wanted to beg him to love her as much as he loved his unborn children. But she wouldn't beg. She wanted to believe their future would be happy. But she couldn't.

All they'd had was sex. If he showed a lack of interest in that, how would she hold him? With the babies? But even that hold would slip away.

Maybe she was getting carried away. After all, they'd just made love that morning before getting out of bed. And every night since she'd returned to their bedroom.

Yes, that was it. She was making a mountain out of a molehill. *Be patient. Take each day as it comes.*

She tried to listen to her own advice the rest of the way into town.

There was only one store in Rawhide that dealt in computers. Janie had discussed the right choice with Brett, and she had decided what to buy. But she wanted to browse first, see if there was anything new on the market.

As they entered the store, her hand still clasped in Pete's, a man hailed them from the back.

"Pete, Janie! What are you doing here? Usually Brett comes in if you need anything." Orry Brownell met them with his hand extended in greeting to Pete. They'd all gone to school together, and Orry had attended their wedding. He'd taken over the hardware store from his dad and updated his merchandise to include computers. From what Janie had heard, it was a booming success.

"We're here to buy a computer, Orry. Janie and me, I mean."

"You, Pete? I sure hope you know what you're doing, Janie. Brett says this guy won't even turn one on."

Janie smiled, but her irritation was growing with those who made Pete sound like an idiot. Just because he wasn't trained in computers didn't mean he couldn't understand. "I'm not worried. We're going to set up his records for the rodeo work."

Realizing he was going to make a sale, Orry got down to business. Janie listened to him and then asked a few questions that had him revising his sales talk.

"Wow. She really knows her stuff," Orry said in an aside to Pete that Janie could clearly hear.

"You're not going to get anywhere with flattery, Orry," she warned him. "I haven't forgotten who pulled my pigtail in kindergarten."

"Aw, Janie, that was years ago. I don't do things like that now."

Janie pointed to a computer and printer. "What's your best price on this combination?"

He quoted her a price and she nodded, making no comment.

"That's really the best I can do."

She smiled and pointed to another. After several quotes, she was about to tell him her decision and ask for a better price, since she wanted the most expensive of the group, when the door to the store opened again.

Casually looking over her shoulder, she froze. Bryan Manning. Just what she needed when everything was going so well.

Orry turned and offered a greeting.

Pete stiffened.

"Pete, please," she whispered.

Bryan, having come in from the bright sunlight, didn't readily identify the other customers until he was almost beside them. Then he flinched and took a step back.

Much to Janie's surprise, Pete extended his hand. "I want to apologize for my behavior the last time we met, Manning. I overreacted."

Warily Bryan shook his hand. "I just want Janie's happiness," he said.

"Me, too. You here to buy a computer?" Pete asked, as if casual conversation with Bryan Manning were something he looked forward to.

Janie stared at her husband.

I was right the first time. Now she knew Pete had lost interest in her. He was showing no jealousy. Instead, he joined in an idle conversation with Bryan. Janie's spirits plummeted, and she wanted to cry. But she struggled to hold back the tears. After all, how could she explain them? She couldn't announce in the middle of a computer store that her husband didn't want her anymore.

She interrupted the chat going on between the three men. "Orry, this is the computer I want, with the printer, but you're going to have to give me a better price. After all, I've picked out the most expensive.''

Orry, with the scent of a sale, immediately gave her his attention. With a great show of reluctance, he mentioned a figure.

"We'll take it," Pete said at once.

"But I think we could get a better deal in Casper," Janie said.

"Yes, you could," Bryan agreed. "I priced this exact same model just last week."

"Damn, you're ganging up on me," Orry complained. "Okay, here's my final offer."

Bryan grinned. "That's the exact price."

Again Pete said, "We'll take it."

"I've got all of it in boxes in the back. Give me half a sec, and I'll bring it out."

After Orry walked away, Pete turned to Bryan. "That was mighty decent of you, Manning. Of course, Orry may never speak to you again."

Bryan smiled. "He won't mind. I've come to buy a new unit for the office, so he'll come out okay." Then Bryan looked at her. "How are you, Janie?"

Janie assured him she was well, but she watched Pete. Not by even a twitch did he show any concern that Bryan was talking to her. What had happened to the jealous husband who'd slugged the man last week?

Orry returned, and Pete pulled out a credit card, telling Janie to gather up whatever supplies she needed. As she did so, Bryan followed her.

"Is everything really all right?" he asked insistently.

Janie turned to stare at him. "Of course it is. Did you think Pete would beat me every night? He's spoiling me rotten, Bryan. I'm very happy."

It heartened her a little to see that Pete was watching them, but he smiled, as if their conversation didn't matter. She hurried over with her purchases.

"This should take care of everything," she assured Pete.

In no time, they loaded their purchases in the pickup and headed back to the ranch.

"That didn't take much time," Pete marveled, smiling at Janie.

"Nope. You can spend a lot of money without even trying."

"If we can get control of all those papers, it will be well worth it."

Janie returned his smile, but she couldn't shake the doubts and fears from her mind. They kept replaying themselves until she thought she would go crazy. But one thought remained constant: Pete hadn't been faking his response each night in their bed.

"Something wrong?"

She looked at Pete in surprise. "No. No, of course not. Everything's fine."

"Is there something else you want? We can go back to town if you do."

"No, there's nothing. We've spent enough money today. But there'll be lots more things to buy for the babies."

Pete looked surprised. "Really? Like what?"

"Clothes, of course, car seats, bottles, diapers, all kinds of things."

"We'll get them all," he promised, and squeezed her hand.

And he would. Anything money could buy, he'd give her. But she wanted his heart.

"LIKE THIS?" Pete asked warily. He pushed the buttons Janie pointed out and watched the screen. Much to his surprise, the program Janie had described appeared on the screen. "Hey, I did it."

"Of course you did. All you needed was someone to show you how."

He leaned over to kiss her. "You can show me how anytime, sweetheart."

"I don't think you're concentrating on the computer."

Pete smothered his sigh and smiled. She was right. He was concentrating on making love to his wife. But he'd have to wait until bedtime.

In the meantime, he had to pay attention to a machine. He hated the whole business, but he was impressed with how fast Janie set it up and began working on his files.

"Are you sure you feel up to this, Janie? You didn't have a nap today. I don't want you to overdo it."

"Maybe I'll go to bed early tonight."

Go to bed early. Magic words. He couldn't wait.

At dinner, Janie bragged about his expertise at the computer. Brett hooted in derision, and Janie launched into him as if he'd insulted Pete's manhood.

"Whoa, Janie!" Pete said. "Brett's been teasing me about computers for at least a decade. That's why

I tease him about his roping. He can't rope a fence post, much less a steer on the move.''

Brett, of course, immediately protested such a scandalous statement. Then Chad and Jake pitched in, and a full-scale, rip-roaring shout-fest took place. Pete, however, kept an eye on Janie. He feared she might be upset, but she'd seen them in action before.

She didn't join in, but she smiled at him.

Megan, on the other hand, appeared stunned.

Pete elbowed Chad and motioned to Megan.

"Honey, what's wrong?" Chad quickly asked her.

She shook her head. "What are you all doing?"

"Aw, don't get upset. This is our version of roughhousing. We're too old to roll around on the floor," Chad explained.

"I see," she said, but she had a bewildered look on her face.

"Don't worry, Megan," Janie assured her. "They don't mean any of it. It's just...exuberant teasing."

Megan's cheeks flushed. "I'm sorry. You see, when my mother began fighting with whichever husband she was with, it was a sign that we were about to move on, to change our lives...." She trailed off, staring at Chad.

"Nope, that's not gonna happen, Meggie," he said, putting his arm around her and pulling her close. "We may fight, even for real, but we're all Randalls. We stick together through thick and thin."

"That's right, Megan," Jake said, his voice earnest.

"It's a four-musketeers mentality," Janie added.

"Six musketeers and growing," Chad said with a grin. "But we've got room for lots more in our house and our hearts, sweetheart, and we will be together forever." He ended his pledge with a kiss that had the others looking in a different direction, albeit with big grins.

Except for Janie.

She studied her tightly clasped hands in her lap. It was painfully obvious that Pete didn't second Chad's assurances. Coming on top of the earlier events of the day, it just underlined to Janie that Pete wasn't sure their marriage would last.

And it broke her heart.

After dinner, the men of the family got into a discussion about pasture management. Janie saw it as an opportune moment to excuse herself. She had something to do before she and Pete went to bed.

PETE WATCHED as Janie went up to bed early, his brow furrowed. Something was wrong. He'd felt a tension growing in Janie all day. Should he go up now?

Jake drew him back into the discussion, unconscious of Pete's indecision. With a sigh, he responded. He loved his brothers. He loved all of them living together. But it did cause some difficulties.

If he and Janie had a house all to themselves, he'd be free to follow her to bed. To demand an explanation. To plead for another chance to make her happy. Hell, he'd spent all afternoon with the stupid computer when he could've been in the saddle. What more did she want?

Almost an hour later, he trudged up the stairs. His gut feeling told him Janie wouldn't let him touch her this evening until whatever was bothering her was settled. He said a fervent prayer that he'd be able to clear it up at once.

With a rueful chuckle, he wondered if God answered prayers for sex. But it was more than that. He needed to hold her. Only when she lay in his arms, sleeping, breathing softly against him, did he believe that she would stay with him. That they had a future.

Tonight, when Chad had promised Megan forever, Pete had wanted so badly to say the same to Janie. But he didn't think she wanted to hear that kind of promise. Not yet.

With a sigh, he prepared himself for an argument and opened the door.

And discovered, once again, that he didn't understand women.

Janie was stretched out on their bed, wearing that silvery negligee she'd rejected on their wedding night. Her hair was unbraided, providing her with a cloak of shining velvet. It even seemed to Pete that she was wearing makeup.

"Janie?" he questioned hoarsely from the door.

"Aren't you coming in, Pete? I've been waiting forever."

It occurred to Pete that Janie was acting out of character. She seldom bothered with makeup even during the day. She'd never played the role of seductress. And she'd never worn anything so shamelessly revealing before.

He should ask her what was wrong.

After struggling several seconds between his conscience and his hormones, he admitted there was no contest. He'd ask questions later.

With his gaze never leaving her, as if he feared she'd disappear if he turned away, he began stripping off his clothes. When he joined her on the bed, her perfume swirled around him, the silk of the negligee enticed him and Janie, all Janie, drove him wild.

A few powerful minutes later, he held her tightly against him and waited until he could speak. The negligee was on the floor, but she lay content against him.

"Janie?" he whispered.

Her eyes were closed. He kissed one eyelid and then the other. "Janie? Are you asleep?"

She mumbled something, as if she was on the edge of drifting off. Pete rubbed his hand up and down her back, loving the silken feel of her skin, and debated his options.

He could awaken her and ask if anything was bothering her. She'd probably think he was crazy. After all, they'd just had the most wonderful sex they'd ever shared. At least, in his opinion.

He had no complaints.

Except that he held a different Janie in his arms. Not that he minded. As long as she wasn't unhappy.

He wanted his Janie to be happy.

Tomorrow. He'd ask her tomorrow if anything was bothering her. That plan satisfied his conscience, and holding her against him satisfied everything else. With a sigh, he fell asleep, too.

As was their Sunday ritual, the next day the Randalls, en masse, attended services at the small church where Pete and Janie had been married. Janie thought their row was the most impressive in the church. Exuding strength and determination, the four Randall men would catch anyone's eye when they were all together.

She and Megan, mixed in among the four men, were a real change. She could remember, as a little girl, watching Pete file into church with his brothers and his father. She'd dreamed of the day he would ask her to sit beside him in their row.

She'd finally achieved that goal.

But she felt dishonest about it. Her seduction scene had worked last evening. Incredibly. But she hadn't been herself. Pete didn't seem to mind or notice, but she had.

She'd vowed to herself that she'd keep Pete's interest, whatever it took. She wouldn't allow him to lose his desire for her. At least not this soon.

What happened when she could no longer use sex to hold him? When the doctor said their lovemaking had to stop because it might damage the babies' health? Or when she grew older and wrinkles appeared around her eyes and her waistline wasn't so trim?

She didn't have an answer to those questions, and it frightened her.

Pete took her hand in his. She smiled at him and then looked away, only to encounter her father's approving smile. Desperately she tried to believe that everything was going to be all right. That Pete, like her father, would remain beside her all her life, even if she couldn't always be beautiful.

And she said a few prayers.

RED INVITED Janie's parents and B.J.'s family to Sunday lunch. He'd put on a pot roast before they'd left for church. Everyone accepted, and dinner was a noisy affair.

Afterward, again B.J., Janie and Megan volunteered to do the dishes. Lavinia and Mildred helped them carry the dishes into the kitchen, but the younger women sent them into the living room to relax.

Janie waited until there was a lull in the conversation before she launched the discussion she wanted.

"Megan, do you have a lot of sexy underwear?"

Her sister-in-law seemed surprised by the question. "Some, I suppose. My mother always believed in that kind of thing, so she would give me negligees for Christmas."

"Oh. I love the one the both of you gave me. Where did you find it?"

B.J. grinned. "We had to drive all the way into Casper to buy it. Rawhide wouldn't have anything that scandalous."

Janie laughed with the other two. "What store?"

"You want some more?" B.J. asked curiously.

"Pete must've liked it," Megan said, grinning.

"Yes, he did. And I thought I might see if they had anything else . . . interesting."

Megan laughed. "Save your money, Janie. If he's anything like Chad, you don't keep it on long enough to get your money's worth."

They all laughed again, but Janie turned away so they wouldn't see the tears pooling in her eyes.

Chapter Sixteen

Pete scratched his head.

Damn if he knew what to do.

"Anything wrong?" Jake asked, riding up beside him.

"Nope, they're moving along just fine," Pete replied, speaking of the cattle he and several cowboys were moving to another pasture.

"I didn't mean the cows."

Pete look at his brother and then turned away. "What are you talking about?"

"I don't know, or I'd ask better questions. It just seems to me that you've been...unsettled the last few days."

Pete sighed. What could he complain of? Great sex? Jake would think he was crazy. "Maybe I have been. This marriage business takes some getting used to."

Jake shifted in his saddle. "Yeah, I guess so. But everything's all right between you and Janie?"

"I guess. But...she's working too hard at it," Pete finally said.

"What do you mean?"

"I don't know!" His frustration burst out of him. "Jake, she's driving me crazy. Every night, like she's putting on a show or something, she seduces me. Hell, the sex is great. But I feel like I've lost the real Janie. She doesn't argue with me anymore. Whatever I say, she agrees. You know that's not like Janie."

"Nope," Jake agreed with a chuckle. "Even when she was little, she could hold her own. Remember when she tipped you into the water tank because you were teasing her?"

Pete laughed with his brother, but Jake's words only increased the feeling that something wasn't right.

"Do you think it's the pregnancy? None of us knows much about that, even if we did read a book."

Pete could feel Jake's eyes on him, and he wished he had an answer. But he didn't. "I don't know. There wasn't anything in the book about someone losing herself...changing into another person. If anything, the book said the mother might get difficult, fussy."

"And she doesn't get that way when it's just the two of you? I'd wondered if living with all of us was too big a strain."

"No, it's not that. We don't talk when it's just the two of us. She goes up early. When I come up, she's ready to lure me into bed." He laughed self-consciously. "Not that she has to try very hard."

"Maybe you should ask her what's wrong."

Pete's cheeks heated up in the cold air. "I've considered that, but the minute I enter the room, my hormones go into overdrive. She even had a new nightgown last night. Some rosy pink thing that was made of a few ribbons and some sheer material." Pete shuddered just thinking of her appearance and his enthusiastic removal of the aforementioned garment.

"I don't know what to tell you, Pete," Jake said, frowning. "Maybe you need to talk to Megan or Lavinia."

Pete stared at his brother in horror. "You want me to tell Lavinia about my sex life with her daughter? Or Megan? Are you crazy?"

Jake laughed. "Sorry. I guess I wasn't thinking. But I don't know what to do to help you."

Jake smiled at his brother. "Don't worry about it, Jake. You can't take care of all our problems for us. I'll work it out . . . one way or another."

THAT NIGHT, Pete watched Janie slip away from the group and start up the stairs. Her steps seemed slower, her tread heavier, than in the past few days. He'd started to ask her several times if she was feeling all right, but in the past she'd always gotten irritated when he worried about her.

Reaching a sudden decision, he broke off the conversation he was having with Brett and got to his feet.

"What's wrong?" Brett asked in surprise.

"Nothing. I have to go upstairs."

Brett grinned. "Are you sure you're leaving her enough time to breathe?"

"What are you talking about?"

"Well, I've heard of nonstop sex, but I've never seen it in action before. You don't hardly let her out of your sight."

Pete started to sit back down, afraid Brett was right, that he'd been hounding Janie. Then he remembered that *she'd* been seducing him. "No, that's not it," he said distractedly, and headed for the stairs.

And it wasn't. He wasn't an animal. He could control his desires...he thought. He'd been prepared to do so when Janie had agreed to marry him. No, it was as he'd told Jake earlier. Something was wrong.

He hoped if he went up when she did, before she transformed herself into his very own painted lady, he could control his hormones and get her to talk to him. Talk had been in short supply lately, at least between the two of them.

Opening the door cautiously, he discovered Janie curled up into a little ball on the far side of the bed.

"Janie? Janie, are you all right?" he asked as he crossed the room and knelt down beside her.

She hid her face from him. "Go away."

He felt her face and found it warm to his touch. "Janie, are you running a fever?"

"No. Go away," she repeated.

"Janie, look at me," Pete commanded sternly. "I need to know if you're sick."

"I'm not sick. But I'm not interested in sex tonight, so you might as well go away. I'll sleep in the other room if you want."

She uncovered her face enough for Pete to see tears streaking down her cheeks.

"Why would you do that?" he asked, fear clutching his heart. "We've been sharing this bed for a while now. There's no reason we can't continue."

"Yes, there is!" she exclaimed, her voice breaking at the end.

Pete rolled back on his heels, staring at her. "What reason?"

"I can't keep this up."

"Keep what up? Janie, are you talking about our marriage? You're not thinking of leaving?" He couldn't keep the horror out of his voice. "You're not leaving, Janie." He may have missed the old Janie, but he wasn't letting either one of them go without a fight.

"Why not?" she cried. "You won't want me anymore."

"What are you talking about?"

"Later," she said with a sniff. "You won't want me later."

"Janie, you're not making any sense."

She sat up on the bed, a look of determination coming over her. "Yes, I am. You just won't admit it. And I'm not waiting around for it to happen." She rolled away from him to the other side of the bed, stood up and ran for the door.

"Janie, what the hell are you talking about?" he shouted, springing to his feet to chase after her. "What is it?"

"You don't love me, and I can't always be young and attractive," she wailed over her shoulder.

She reached the stairs while she was answering Pete's question and missed the first step. In horror,

Pete watched her fall, as if in slow motion, and roll down the stairs.

"Janie!" Fear filled him as he raced down after her.

She lay silent on the floor.

The rest of the family came running out at the commotion.

"Janie," Pete crooned, lifting her up against his chest. "Janie, talk to me."

Jake snapped out orders. "Brett, call the doc. Chad, go get B.J."

"B.J.?" Chad asked. "She's an animal doctor."

"She's also the only female to have had a baby around here. Go get her." Then he turned his attention to Pete and Janie. "Did she break anything?"

Pete stared at him, a dazed look in his eyes.

Jake ran his hands over Janie's arms and legs. "Nope, I don't think so."

Pete held his wife against him, as if trying to share his strength with her. He didn't even notice the others around him.

"Pete, can you carry her to bed? With nothing broken, I think it will be okay to move her." Jake had to tell him a second time, but finally Pete heard him.

"I can carry her," he assured him gruffly, trying to hold back the tears that filled him. He couldn't bear the thought of Janie hurt.

He stood and lifted Janie high against his chest. With Jake at his back, as if offering support, he started up the stairs.

"Megan," Jake called over his shoulder, "as soon as Brett finishes talking to the doctor, maybe you'd better call Lavinia and Hank."

Jake hurried around Pete and his burden to strip back the covers on their bed. "We'd better keep her warm. She might go into shock."

Pete laid her down, reluctant to let go of her. He had the feeling that as long as he held her, she would be okay.

"Pete, you want to take off her shoes?"

He turned to stare at Jake, a blank look on his face. What had Jake said?

"Her shoes, Pete. Take off her shoes."

He did so and then drew the covers over Janie just as the bedroom door opened. B.J., with Chad right behind her, came into the room.

"How is she?"

"She hasn't regained consciousness yet," Jake said in a low voice.

B.J. gently moved Pete aside and felt Janie's pulse. Then she opened one of her eyes. After that, she gently patted Janie's cheek. "Janie? Janie, can you hear me?"

Pete wanted to protest. But Janie's groaned response stopped him. He pushed closer. "Janie? Are you okay? Janie, speak to me."

"My head," she said with a low moan.

"Doc Jacoby is on his way, Janie," B.J. assured her calmly. "Just lie still and rest."

Janie clutched her stomach instead. "Ooh!"

"Are you having pains, Janie?" B.J. asked, her voice again calm.

"My babies!" Janie cried, sending a chill through the room.

PETE PACED THE FLOOR, unable to contain himself. Doc, Lavinia and B.J. had been upstairs with Janie for at least half an hour. The fear that he might lose her so consumed him that he didn't hear footsteps coming down the stairs.

Perhaps it was the concerted movement of the rest of his family that alerted him. By the time he turned around, Doc was almost to the bottom.

"Janie...?" he asked painfully.

"She's going to be fine. She has a mild concussion, and there will be an assortment of bumps and bruises, but nothing serious."

Pete bowed his head in relief.

"And the babies?" Jake asked softly.

Pete's head snapped up in time to see the doctor let out a long sigh. "I don't know. We'll know more after twenty-four hours."

"You mean she might lose the babies?" Pete asked in horror.

"I hope not. Babies are well cushioned. But I'm not promising anything right now. Lavinia is going to stay with her tonight. I'll be out first thing in the morning to check her again."

"You're not moving her to a hospital?" Jake asked.

"Nope. Lavinia is almost as good as Priddy. Janie will be better off here." He turned to Pete again. "You can go see her for a minute or two, but don't upset her."

Uncertainty and fear filled him. He was the reason she'd fallen in the first place. He'd already upset her. What if the sight of him disturbed her all over again?

With a nod to the doctor, he started up the stairs. He couldn't *not* see her. He had to see with his own eyes that she was all right. But he was afraid his presence wouldn't make her feel better.

"Lavinia?" he whispered from the door to the bedroom. "Doc said I could see her for a minute or two."

She motioned for him to come in. "Janie, Pete's here to see you."

Even Pete, from across the room, could see her body flinch at her mother's words. He and Lavinia exchanged looks of concern, but he walked to Janie's bedside.

"Sweetheart, I'm sorry. I didn't mean to argue with you." He could feel Lavinia's gaze on him, but it was no time to be dishonest. "I'll do whatever you want, I promise."

Even if it meant watching her leave. He wanted her—forever—but most of all, he wanted her safe and happy. Even if she went away. Or married someone else. But the thought of it was tearing him in two.

He brushed her lips with his, gently, softly, and then, without another word, left the room.

BY THE NEXT EVENING, Doc assured Pete the babies were fine, as would be Janie after some rest. While the relief was incredible, Pete's heart was heavy.

He was sure Janie intended to leave. She'd asked her mother to stay another night with her, after the doctor refused to allow her to go back to her parents' home.

He visited Janie once that evening, but she scarcely responded to him. As he left the room, Lavinia gave him a sad smile.

Yes, Janie was leaving.

"YOU CAN'T GO without telling him why," Lavinia said, frustration in her voice. "Janie, the man has been distraught with worry. He cares about you."

"He cares about his babies," Janie replied softly, one hand cradling her stomach. The scare she'd received, endangering her babies' lives, had made them so much more precious. And helped her make some decisions.

Unfortunately her mother was right. She couldn't leave Pete without telling him...without assuring him of a role in his children's lives.

"All right, Mom. We'll wait for him to come back."

"He's downstairs in the kitchen right now."

"He didn't ride out today?"

"Of course not. He's waiting to do whatever he can to help you."

Janie's eyes filled with tears, and she turned away. "Ask him to come up."

She moved to the window, hoping the bright winter sun would dry out her eyes. Reminded of that first meeting with Pete after she'd found out she was pregnant, Janie dug deep for the control she'd had then. She refused to let Pete know how painful this meeting would be for her.

"Janie."

That low, sexy voice that thrilled her announced Pete's arrival.

She didn't turn around. "Pete, I'm going back home."

Silence greeted her announcement, but she didn't realize he'd moved until his hands fell on her shoulders and gently turned her around. "Why?"

She wasn't prepared to answer that question. "I won't keep you from seeing the babies or—or being their daddy."

"Why, Janie? Is it Manning?"

That question brought her gaze to his, filled with indignation. "Of course not!"

"Then why can't you stay? Why can't you let me take care of you? I'll sleep on the daybed if you want."

She ducked her head. "Pete, I can't continue to— I'd be living a lie."

"You once said you loved me."

Her heart contracted in pain. Once? She would always love this stubborn man. "Yes," she whispered.

"Janie, I'll try harder. I'll do whatever you want," he pleaded softly. "Give me another chance."

The tears reappeared, and she gasped, trying to hold them back. "Pete, it's me, not you."

He lifted her chin, staring at her, a frown on his face. One tear escaped and traveled down her cheek, and he erased it with his thumb. "What are you talking about, Janie?"

She tried to turn away, but he wouldn't let her. Finally she lifted her gaze to his and told him the truth.

"I tried to be sexy," she explained with a hiccup, "but I can't hold you with sex the rest of my life. I won't always be attractive or young. And I can't live with the fear that you'll find someone else who is."

As if they were frozen in a lovers' tableau, they stood there, Pete's arms around her, their faces lifted to each other. Suddenly Pete lifted her in his arms and spun around.

"Dear God, give me strength," she heard him mutter.

"Pete, what are you doing?" she shrieked.

"Sorry, sweetheart, I forgot about your concussion," he muttered as he set her back down on her feet. Then, to her surprise, he tried to kiss her.

She shoved him away. "Pete, I'm leaving, remember?"

"Nope. Not in a million years."

"Pete Randall, you can't order me around. I'll do what I jolly well please, and you can just—"

He threw back his head in laughter, and she stared at him in surprise. Had he gone crazy?

"That's my Janie," he said as he chuckled. "I've missed you so much."

"What are you talking about?"

"Janie, the sex has been incredible these last few days—"

"I know, Pete, but I can't—"

"Would you let me finish?"

Irritation rose at his high-handedness, but she nodded grudgingly.

"Since when did I ever need seducing?" he asked, a grin on his face.

"When you began losing interest."

He looked as if she'd poleaxed him. "What?"

"You stopped wanting me all the time."

"Janie Dawson Randall, I have never stopped wanting you every minute of every day since the first time I made love to you. And I never will."

"What about the day we bought the computer?"

He shook his head in bewilderment. "What about it?"

"You acted like you wanted to make love to me before we left for shopping."

"I did. That doesn't prove I don't want you."

"But you didn't."

"You said I'd mess up your makeup!" he exploded.

"Such a silly excuse wouldn't have stopped you in the past. And—and..." She paused to restrain her tears. "And you were friendly with Bryan."

He leaned his forehead against hers. "Are you out of your mind, Janie? Do I have to punch out every man who even looks at you for you to believe I want you?"

She buried her face in his chest. "It doesn't matter, Pete," she said wearily. "I won't always look this way. Someone younger, prettier, will come along. I'm not strong enough to face that."

"Janie," Pete whispered, raising her head again, "I think I forgot to tell you something."

She blinked several times, wanting to ask if he'd already found someone else, but she couldn't bring herself to do so.

"What?"

"I forgot to tell you that I love you."

She stared at him. The words she'd always wanted to hear were now impossible to believe. "Pete, please—"

"Janie, I've always loved you. Only you. But at first, I was afraid to tell you, afraid to admit how much I needed you. Then, after we married, you seemed...unhappy with me. I realized how much I loved you, but I thought I had to—to woo you back. To convince you to love me again. So I was trying to do whatever would make you happy." He grinned. "Like spend all afternoon using that stupid computer."

"You didn't like it?" she asked, distracted by his hands. They were stroking her back in a rhythmic pattern.

"I hated it. I know computers are good, but I won't want to mess with them. I'd rather my wife take care of that end of our business."

"I could do that but, Pete—"

His lips covered hers before she could finish. The magic of his touch was still there even when she thought she was leaving him. When he lifted his mouth from hers, she tried again. "Pete, I'm not sure—"

He kissed her again.

This time he spoke. "I'm sure, Janie. I'm sure with all my heart. There will never be anyone else to tempt me. And I don't need a sexy lady every night. Even a crabby Janie will do me."

"Are you sure, because I can't—"

He silenced her with his lips. "I missed you, sweetheart."

"What?"

"The last few days, I knew you weren't being yourself. I wanted to argue with you just to find the old Janie. But every time I opened the bedroom door, well, other parts of me took over."

"Really, Pete? You're sure?"

"I'm more sure of my love for you than anything else in the world."

In a small voice, she said, "I was afraid if I lost the babies you wouldn't want to be married to me anymore." She felt ashamed to admit such a thing, but she wanted to be honest. If—and she still wasn't sure—happiness was there waiting, within her reach, she didn't want it tainted with unresolved issues.

He tightened his embrace. "Janie, I would've grieved for our babies if we'd lost them. But you... I couldn't survive without you. Don't ever leave me."

Finally he'd convinced her. She had found the love she'd been seeking when she'd first come into his arms. And now she'd never have to leave them.

After several minutes of reassuring each other, Janie gasped.

"What is it, sweetheart?" Pete asked with concern.

"Mom! I told her I was leaving you. We'd better go tell her."

"Good idea. Besides, if we don't get away from this bed, I may not be able to restrain myself, and I think it's too soon after your accident."

"Probably. At least until nap time this afternoon," she said with a grin.

They walked arm in arm down the stairs to the kitchen. When they opened the door, they found the full complement of Randalls, along with her mother, waiting for them, apprehension on their faces.

Janie let her husband speak for her. He beamed at their audience and simply said, "We love each other."

Everyone circled them, kissing Janie's cheek and patting Pete on the back. Relief and excitement filled the room.

Brett, after everyone sat back down, chuckled. "*I* could've told you that."

"Don't be too sure," Pete warned. "Love isn't as easy as it looks."

"And it's about time you found out," Jake added. "After all, you caught Janie's bouquet, remember?"

"Yeah, but I'm going to always be the bridesmaid," Brett joked.

"Uh-uh," Jake said, rubbing his chin. "We'll see."

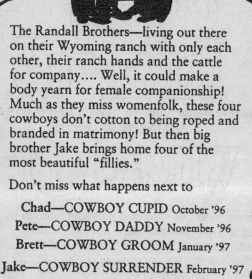

The collection of the year!
NEW YORK TIMES BESTSELLING AUTHORS

Linda Lael Miller
Wild About Harry

Janet Dailey
Sweet Promise

Elizabeth Lowell
Reckless Love

Penny Jordan
Love's Choices

and featuring
Nora Roberts
The Calhoun Women

This special trade-size edition features four of the wildly
popular titles in the Calhoun miniseries together in
one volume—a true collector's item!

Pick up these great authors and a chance to win
a weekend for two in New York City at the
Marriott Marquis Hotel on Broadway! We'll pay
for your flight, your hotel—even a Broadway show!

Available in December at your favorite retail outlet.

Bestselling Author

RACHEL LEE

Dares you to make

A FATEFUL CHOICE

For Jennifer Fox, there is just one escape from the suffering she's felt each day since her husband and children were killed in a plane crash—a plane she was supposed to be on. She wants to die. And she's willing to hire her own killer. As an attorney, she knows there are men who will do anything for a price. Rook Rydell isn't one of them. He wants nothing to do with Jennifer's death wish…but he's her only chance to stay alive.

Look for A FATEFUL CHOICE this November, at your favorite retail outlet.

MIRA The brightest star in women's fiction

MRLAFC

Merry Christmas, Baby!

A romantic collection filled with the magic of Christmas and the joy of children.

SUSAN WIGGS, Karen Young and Bobby Hutchinson bring you Christmas wishes, weddings and romance, in a charming trio of stories that will warm up your holiday season.

MERRY CHRISTMAS, BABY! also contains Harlequin's special gift to you—a set of FREE GIFT TAGS included in every book.

Brighten up your holiday season with *MERRY CHRISTMAS, BABY!*

Available in November at your favorite retail store.

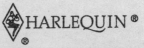

HARLEQUIN ®

MCB

1997
Reader's Engagement Book
A calendar of important dates and anniversaries for readers to use!

Informative and entertaining—with notable dates and trivia highlighted throughout the year.

Handy, convenient, pocketbook size to help you keep track of your own personal important dates.

Added bonus—contains $5.00 worth of coupons for upcoming Harlequin and Silhouette books. This calendar more than pays for itself!

Available beginning in November at your favorite retail outlet.

HARLEQUIN ®   Silhouette®

◆HARLEQUIN®

Don't miss these Harlequin favorites by some of our most distinguished authors! And now you can receive a discount by ordering two or more titles!

HT#25657	PASSION AND SCANDAL by Candace Schuler	$3.25 U.S ☐ $3.75 CAN. ☐	
HP#11787	TO HAVE AND TO HOLD by Sally Wentworth	$3.25 U.S. ☐ $3.75 CAN. ☐	
HR#03385	THE SISTER SECRET by Jessica Steele	$2.99 U.S. ☐ $3.50 CAN ☐	
HS#70634	CRY UNCLE by Judith Arnold	$3.75 U.S. ☐ $4.25 CAN. ☐	
HI#22346	THE DESPERADO by Patricia Rosemoor	$3.50 U.S. ☐ $3.99 CAN ☐	
HAR#16610	MERRY CHRISTMAS, MOMMY by Muriel Jensen	$3.50 U.S. ☐ $3.99 CAN. ☐	
HH#28895	THE WELSHMAN'S WAY by Margaret Moore	$4.50 U.S. ☐ $4.99 CAN. ☐	

(limited quantities available on certain titles)

AMOUNT	$
DEDUCT: 10% DISCOUNT FOR 2+ BOOKS	$
POSTAGE & HANDLING	$
($1.00 for one book, 50¢ for each additional)	
APPLICABLE TAXES*	$_____
TOTAL PAYABLE	$_____
(check or money order—please do not send cash)	

To order, complete this form and send it, along with a check or money order for the total above, payable to Harlequin Books, to: **In the U.S.:** 3010 Walden Avenue, P.O. Box 9047, Buffalo, NY 14269-9047; **In Canada:** P.O. Box 613, Fort Erie, Ontario, L2A 5X3.

Name: _____

Address: _____ City: _____

State/Prov.: _____ Zip/Postal Code: _____

*New York residents remit applicable sales taxes.
  Canadian residents remit applicable GST and provincial taxes.   HBACK-OD3

Look us up on-line at: http://www.romance.net